Wedding Weekend

REBECCA TALLEY

DUBON PUBLISHING

Chapter One

Eden Brooks exited the plane and walked across Valley International Airport with her rolling suitcase trailing behind her. Stepping outside into the warm afternoon Texas air was a stark contrast to the cooler temperatures she'd left behind in Oregon. At the curb, she located the shuttle to South Padre Island.

"I'm going to the Diamond Resort," she said to the driver, who wore his dark hair in a single ponytail.

"First time to the island?" he said over his shoulder.

"No, I came here once for spring break back in college. My old roommate, and best friend, is getting married Saturday on the beach. At sunset." As the words left her mouth, she couldn't help but envy the romance of it. Exchanging vows with the ocean and the setting sun in the background, how much more romantic could it get? Sophie was beyond lucky, especially because finding a good man was nearly impossible. But Sophie had found a great one in Antonio.

The drive took over an hour, which gave her plenty of time to catch her breath and relax. She hadn't seen Sophie in a year, but they'd kept in touch on social media and through phone calls and texts. Sophie had met Antonio during their junior year at UT in Austin, and six years later, they were finally tying the knot near Sophie's hometown of Brownsville, Texas.

"I forgot about that huge bridge," Eden said as they approached the island with the massive structure ahead of them.

"The resort is the tallest building over there." He pointed across the bridge.

"Oh, I see it." The white building was easy to spot against the deep blue sky.

"It's a popular destination. Right on the beach. Large pool with a restaurant and bar next to the water," he said. "You'll like it."

"We're all coming in today for a long weekend." She was excited to spend time with Sophie, then witness her marriage.

"You should check out the dolphin trips or the snorkeling. There's also a dinner cruise and a pirate ship."

"Pirate ship?" They hadn't seen that during spring break. Eden hoped they'd have some time to explore the island.

"Appeals to the kids." He laughed. "Took my son there a few weeks ago."

"Sounds interesting." She tried to imagine what it might look like inside a pirate ship.

"We also have concerts." He gestured with his hand. "I think the Goo Goo Dolls are here Friday Night at Fisherman Jack's Outdoor Bar."

"There's a lot to do here." Eden was sure Sophie had everything already planned out.

The shuttle bus pulled up to the hotel. "Here we are," the driver said.

"Thank you. And thanks for the information about things to do here. I'm hoping to have some down time and relax." Relaxing would be a welcome change to her hectic, stressful schedule back in Oregon.

"I hope you enjoy it here. Maybe you will find some romance at the wedding?" He winked.

"Uh, I don't think so." Eden wasn't here to meet a man.

He handed her the suitcase. "Never discount what can happen at a weekend wedding, especially here on the island." He said it in such a mystical way Eden had to do a double take. Was he serious? This weekend was all about Sophie. Her wedding. Her weekend.

Eden checked into her room. It was spacious and looked out over the Gulf. The salty sea air floated around her room. She kicked off her wedges and collapsed onto the bed.

A knock sounded, so she got up and opened the door.

"Sophie," she screamed. The two friends hugged each other and took turns squealing.

"You look fabulous," Sophie said. "What did you do to your hair?"

"It's called bronde. Do you like it?"

"Oh, I love it. The blonde ends are so beautiful." Sophie said, her dark brown eyes wide. "And you look like Blake Lively's twin."

Eden laughed. She could only wish she looked like a glamorous celebrity. "Enough about me." She waved her hand. "You are going to be a gorgeous bride. You look so fit."

Sophie flexed her bicep. "I've faithfully gone to the gym every day for a year."

"Every day? That's impressive. I'm happy if I ever make to the gym." She wanted to go, but the kids she placed in homes had to take precedence over trips to the gym.

"Okay, not every single day, but close. My dress is strapless and I want to look good." Sophie smoothed her long dark hair.

"You definitely will." Eden gave Sophie another hug. "I've missed you."

"I've missed you too. I'm so happy you're here." Sophie squeezed Eden.

Eden stepped back and peered at her best friend since college. "I wouldn't have missed this for anything. You've been planning it forever."

"I know, right?" Sophie chuckled. "It's about time we finally got married."

Feeling exhausted, Eden sat on the edge of the bed. "Did Antonio's grandparents make it?"

"Yes." Sophie sat in the gray upholstered chair by the window.

"I remember him talking about them. I bet he's glad they're here." Dozens of memories shot through Eden's mind.

"He is. I think his dad might show up, but who knows? I'm not going to let him ruin the weekend." Sophie slung her legs over the arm of the chair.

"What are the plans?" Eden pulled her hair up into a messy bun on the top of her head. It felt good to relax with Sophie. It had been too long since they'd been together.

Sophie's eyes lit up and she clasped her hands together. "Tonight, the bridal party is having dinner."

"The rehearsal dinner?" Eden leaned back on her elbows. If she had her way, she and Sophie would stay in her room and talk all night like they used to back in school.

"Not the rehearsal dinner. It's a casual one with the groomsmen and the bridesmaids." Sophie gave a sly smile.

"No." Eden shook her head.

"What? I didn't even say anything," Sophie said, feigning innocence, but Eden could see right through her.

"I know what's going on in that head of yours." Eden sat up.

With mocked indignation, Sophie said, "You do?"

"Remember, I told you—" Eden held her hand up "—I don't want you to try to fix me up."

"Why not?" Sophie blinked a few times.

"Because I'm not into flings." That kind of thing wasn't at all enticing to Eden.

Sophie pointed at her. "I know that. I'm not talking about a fling."

"Your relationship with Antonio is awesome, but it's rare. Definitely not the norm. After what I've seen with my job, I'm a little . . ."

"Cynical?" Sophie said with a tilt of her head.

"That sounds pretty harsh." Eden paused for a moment. "Maybe doubtful. Extremely doubtful."

"But Antonio and I have something amazing."

"You do, but I've seen so many broken women and destroyed relationships, I think—"

"I get that. But you can't give up on love." Sophie smiled. "And Jeremy is so great. He's sweet and fun. And so handsome. Not as handsome as Antonio, of course." She laughed. "I just want you to find someone and be as happy as I am."

"I think the two of you sucked all the happiness out of the atmosphere for the next several years." Eden stood and walked over to her suitcase.

"Antonio is so wonderful." Sophie gave a dramatic sigh.

Eden hefted her suitcase onto the bed and unzipped it. "Who knew the guy in your anatomy class would end up being your husband."

"I did." Sophie giggled. "The moment I saw him I knew. Remember?"

Eden smiled at the memory of that day when Sophie was so sure she'd found her Mr. Right. "Yeah, But I didn't think you would really marry him."

"It was love at first sight for me." Sophie fanned herself.

Eden shook her head. She believed in attraction at first sight, but love was something you developed over time and through experiences. "That's not a thing."

"But it is. I'm proof of it." Sophie patted her chest.

Eden wasn't going to argue. "Well, I'm very happy for you. And I'm glad you're getting married."

"Me, too." Sophie jumped to her feet. "Now let's go to dinner."

"Can I change my clothes? I'm not used to warmer temperatures. It was cold and drizzly when I left Portland."

"Sure." Sophie glanced at her phone. "Meet us down in the lobby in thirty minutes?"

"Yep," Eden said as she opened the door for Sophie.

After Sophie left, Eden decided to take a quick shower. She put on a light floral dress and found her strappy sandals—a perfect combination for dinner on South Padre Island. She brushed through her hair, put on some lip gloss, and dabbed some perfume on her neck.

Eden took the elevator down to the lobby. When the doors opened she saw Sophie surrounded by a group of people. She walked over to the group. Sophie spotted her and slung her arm around her. "You look beautiful, as usual."

Eden smiled. Sophie always made her feel good.

A man with his back to her turned around and it made Eden take a sudden breath. His bronzed skin, thick dark hair, and chocolate brown eyes made her pulse quicken. He. Was. Gorgeous.

Chapter Two

"This is Jeremy Rivera," Sophie said with a quirked eyebrow. "Jeremy, this is my college roommate and best friend, Eden Brooks."

"Nice to meet you," he said in a voice that was so rich and smooth it was like Dove dark chocolate. He extended his hand.

When Eden took it, a tingle of energy rushed up her arm. "You too," she said as casually as possible.

Sophie smiled at her with an I-told-you-so expression on her face.

"I think everyone is here," Antonio said as he approached them. "Oh, hey, Eden. So good to see you." He hugged her.

"You look as handsome as ever," Eden said. "Congratulations. I'm so happy for both of you."

Antonio leaned over and kissed Sophie on the cheek. "I'm a lucky man."

"I'm the lucky one," Sophie cooed.

"You two are meant for each other," Eden said, trying not to be too envious of the perfect couple.

"Let's get this celebration started," Sophie said with a wide grin. "We're having dinner here in the hotel restaurant, so follow us." Sophie and Antonio walked hand-in-hand toward the glass doors and the group fell in line behind them.

Sophie insisted that Eden sit next to Jeremy.

"Where do you live?" he asked, his brown eyes drawing her in.

"Oregon." She sipped her lemon water. "Portland, actually."

He smiled, exposing brilliant white teeth that belonged in a toothpaste commercial. "I love Portland. My sister lives there, so I've visited several times. Beautiful place. Very eclectic. And weird."

Eden laughed. "Yep. 'Keep Portland Weird' is our favorite slogan. I moved there right after college in Austin, which, incidentally has as its slogan, 'Keep Austin Weird.'"

"I guess you like weird cities?" He laughed.

Eden shrugged, then smiled.

Jeremy leaned in and a whiff of his woodsy cologne floated past her nose. "So, Eden who likes weird cities, what do you do in Portland?"

"I'm a social worker." Usually, men didn't want to know much about her job.

He gazed at her. "Interesting. What are your responsibilities?"

Intrigued that he wanted to know more, she said, "I place children in foster homes."

He studied her. "That must be a difficult job."

She nodded. "It is. Very emotional at times. I try to stay focused on the kids and what's best for them."

"I've never met a social worker before, but that says a lot about you."

"It does?" She'd never had anyone say that before.

He smiled with his million-dollar smile again. "Yeah. You obviously care about people, especially children. I'd guess you have a pretty big heart."

Eden felt the heat rise in her cheeks.

"You have an honorable profession. One that really makes a difference."

Eden cleared her throat. She suddenly wanted to know more about the handsome man who sat next to her. "Tell me about you."

"Not a lot to tell." He sat back. "I live in Dallas. That's where I met Antonio. We work for the same software company, which makes me a computer nerd." He laughed.

Nerd was not the word Eden would've used to describe him. At all.

"Okay, everyone, we want y'all to enjoy dinner and get to know each other. We hope this weekend will be as awesome for all of you as it will be for us," Antonio said. "We're glad you're here with us."

"I'm looking forward to the festivities," Jeremy said. "Antonio has been so distracted the last few months."

"They have the real deal." Eden watched Antonio and Sophie exchange a look, then share a tender kiss. She sighed inwardly. "Not many people get to have that."

Jeremy sipped his drink. "Antonio says it was love at first sight. You believe in that kind of thing?"

"Not really." She had to be honest. Sophie might have had a fairy tale, but that wasn't life for regular people.

"Me either. I think they are some fluke of nature." He smiled and her stomach flip-flopped.

"I'd like to make a toast to my beautiful bride," Antonio said.

Sophie looked at him with love-filled eyes.

"To the woman who captured my heart. I can't wait to marry you because you make every day worth living."

Audible ooh and ahhs came from the women in the group.

"You are so sweet," Sophie said, then turned to the group. "I won the lottery with this one."

"Have they always been this way?" Jeremy asked.

"Ever since they met. I remember her coming back to our apartment and going on and on about this great guy in her class." A twinge of something nudged Eden. Watching Sophie and Antonio made her almost believe she could find the same kind of love. Almost.

"I hear we're going to have a great time." He nodded. "It'll be like a mini-vacation."

Eden laughed. "Vacation? What's that?" She hadn't taken any time off in the last two years.

"Right? Who has time for one of those?" He took a swig of his drink.

"I guess we're both having a vacation whether we want to or not." Eden smiled.

Jeremy peered at her. "I'm okay with that." He raised an eyebrow and gave her a slight smile. Eden's heart jumped to her throat.

"Me too," she answered.

They ate their dinners and chatted about their favorite movies, weather in Texas, and if the Longhorns or the Aggies were the better team. Since Eden was a University of Texas alum she argued that the best team was obviously the Longhorns.

"Now that we're done with dinner," Sophie said, "we're going to relax at the pool and hot tub. Everyone needs to change and meet back down here."

"See you at the pool?" Jeremy said.

Eden nodded.

Once they were in the elevator, Sophie said, "Looks like you two are hitting it off. You're welcome." Sophie giggled.

Eden rolled her eyes, then pursed her lips to stifle a smile.

Sophie turned to her. "He's great, isn't he?"

"Yeah." He seemed to be pretty awesome, but Eden knew well enough from her job that not everything is as it seems, especially concerning relationships.

"But?" Sophie narrowed her eyes.

"No but."

"Eden?"

She didn't want to be a downer on Sophie's wedding weekend, but she knew her best friend would continue to badger her, so she decided to say what was on her mind. "Look, you and Antonio have something really special. Most of us don't find that. Believe me, I've seen enough heartbreak and sadness to last a lifetime."

"I know you see a lot of bad stuff with your job, but that doesn't mean you can't find a great guy," Sophie said with confidence.

"Maybe it'll be fun to hang out with Jeremy for the weekend, but nothing will ever come of it. Even if, and that's a huge if, we hit it off in a big way, we live way too far away from each other anyway. So, let's enjoy the weekend and you worry about your wedding, not about me." Eden couldn't be any clearer than that.

Sophie gave her a disappointed look. "You can't blame me for hoping."

"I know. You want me to be happy like you." She couldn't be mad at Sophie for wanting her to find a good man like Antonio.

There weren't very many men like him, at least not in Eden's experience.

Sophie threaded her arm through Eden's. "I do want you to find someone amazing."

"Maybe. Someday."

After they left the elevator, Eden went to her room and dug through her suitcase. She pulled out her suit. Eden hadn't been in a swimsuit in months. Maybe years. She couldn't remember the last time she'd gone swimming. Her job kept her way too busy. In fact, she couldn't remember the last time she'd taken any time off. Most of the time, she brought her work home, worrying about the kids with whom she worked. Too many kids were in the foster system, and she wished more parents would provide safe, secure homes for their children.

Eden shook her head. She needed to not worry about the kids, but focus on Sophie. This was her special weekend.

"I wish I'd done five thousand crunches this week." Eden looked at herself in the bathroom mirror. "I need to add working out to my schedule." *Yeah, that's not going to happen.*

A knock sounded. "Are you ready? Came Sophie's voice through the door.

Eden opened the door.

"Dang, you look good. And let me guess. You still don't work out or anything." Sophie shook her head.

"I don't have time."

"You are the girl the rest of us love to hate—thin and beautiful and don't even have to work at it."

"Thanks, Sophie."

Sophie threw her arms around Eden. "I'm so happy you're here. I was worried you wouldn't be able to come."

"Are you kidding? Nothing would keep me from your wedding. After all, I listened to you night after night about Antonio for how long? It's only fitting I get to see you marry him. Finally." Memories of late night talks about guys rushed through Eden's mind. Her topic of choice changed regularly, but Sophie's was always about Antonio. They seemed to be fated to be together.

"Finally is right. I can't wait." Sophie grinned.

"Are the other girls ready?" Eden asked.

"Yes. They all went down already. I guess we were taking too long to look hot in our suits." Sophie laughed.

"The other girls are your cousins, right?" Eden had met one of the girls one time when she went to visit Sophie in Brownsville, but she didn't know the rest of the bridesmaids.

Sophie nodded. "Yep. My cousins. But fair warning. I'm gonna throw my bouquet right at you, so be ready to catch it."

"Soph, I don't think anyone on this planet can ever be as happy as you are right now."

Sophie clapped her hands together. "This is going to be the best weekend ever."

Eden and Sophie walked out of the hotel lobby. The expansive pool had a waterfall at one end and a hot tub at the other. A restaurant was adjacent to the pool. Eden scanned the area and spotted the wedding group. "There they are," she said.

Sophie started waving and Antonio jumped out of the pool and rushed over. "Hey, baby." He gave her a kiss.

"Eden is looking for Jeremy," Sophie said with a smile.

"No, I'm not." She wished Sophie would stop trying to be a matchmaker. Eden was more than capable of finding herself a man. She didn't have one right now because she didn't want one. She was too busy trying to mop up the messes resulting from disintegrated relationships.

"I saw him over there." Antonio pointed toward the hot tub.

Eden casually looked over and saw Jeremy talking to a woman. When the woman turned, it was one of the bridesmaids.

"Oh, he's with Alicia," Sophie said. "But she's way too young for him. And not his type. I'm sure he wants to see you, Eden."

"Actually, I'm not getting in the hot tub yet. I need to check my messages." It was a good excuse because it was true. Eden was worried about a couple of placements and needed to make sure everything was okay back home.

"No work while you're here." Sophie wagged her finger.

"I only need to check a couple of things."

Sophie put her hand on her hips. "But then promise to come over to the hot tub."

"I will."

Sophie snuggled up to Antonio and they left.

Eden sat at a small table and called up her email. Over the top of her phone she watched Jeremy and Alicia. It looked as though they were deep in conversation. Alicia laughed as she let her head fall back, then she put her arm around him. Obviously, she was interested in him. Which was fine. Because Eden wasn't. She was here to support Sophie and that was it.

"Can I get you something to eat or drink?" a short woman with blonde hair asked.

"I just had dinner, but I think I could still fit in an order of fries."

The woman left and Eden let her gaze return to the hot tub. Jeremy and Alicia were still talking. Alicia was very animated as she spoke to him. Eden turned her chair so she wouldn't be tempted to keep watching them, because it made her feel like a stalker.

She read through several emails on her phone hoping that nothing needed her immediate attention. Then she spotted one from a co-worker about a child Eden had placed in foster care last week.

Someone cleared his throat. Eden turned and there stood Jeremy, water dripping off his large shoulders, cut biceps, and toned abs. *Did the temperature rise ten degrees?*

"Hi," he said.

"Hi." She put down her phone so she didn't appear to be rude.

The waitress brought over the fries. "Here's your order." She set it in front of Eden, which made her feel a little self-conscious. "And here's some ketchup. Anything else?" the waitress asked.

"Thank you. I think I'm fine now."

Jeremy sat at the table, his thick hair still wet and slicked back to expose his mesmerizing eyes. "I see you're into health food." He laughed.

Eden shrugged. Besides her chocolate obsession, she didn't normally eat junk food, except when it came to a delectable plate of fries.

Jeremy reached over and stole a fry. "Are you going to come in the hot tub?"

She pointed at her phone. "I need to answer an email."

He studied her. "Are you always on the clock?" He took another fry and dipped it in ketchup, then slipped it into his mouth.

Trying to focus on his words instead of his lips, Eden said, "I guess you could say that. It's pretty tough when I have to place children in foster homes. I don't like to break up families, but sometimes it's in the best interest of the kids to take them out of the home. It's hard for everyone. I need to be available to help if I'm needed."

Jeremy leaned in and peered at her. "What made you want to go into social work?"

The intensity of his gaze made Eden shift her weight. "When I was a kid, one of my friends had a terrible home life. Renee came and lived with us for several months while her mom tried to get sober. Her dad wasn't around and Renee desperately wanted a stable family. She often told me that she wanted to change places with me. She ended up moving in with her grandparents in another state and we lost touch, but she made such an impression on me that I decided I wanted to help others like her."

"That's awesome." Jeremy smiled and it made her stomach quiver.

Eden took a fry and bit into the soft, salty potato. "What about you? Did you always want to be a computer nerd?"

He shrugged. "It wasn't my dream, but I'm good with computers."

"What was your dream?" She was intrigued.

A timid expression crossed his face. He played with a fry. "I wanted to be a professional musician."

A musician? This man was full of surprises. "Oh yeah? What instrument do you play?"

He sat back with a slight smile. "Piano, guitar, fiddle. And the drums."

"Wow. Why didn't you pursue a career in music?" He played so many instruments it seemed like being a professional musician was a no-brainer.

"Not very practical, as my mom reminded me often." An expression flashed across his face too quickly for Eden to interpret it.

"Do you sing?" she asked.

He bit into another French fry. "Yeah, and I write songs."

Eden hadn't ever met someone who wrote songs. This man seemed to be all sorts of contradictions. Not at all what she'd assumed about him. "What kinds of songs?"

He looked at her with a sparkle in his eyes. "All kinds."

"I'd love to hear one." She couldn't think of anything else she'd rather do at the moment than listen to him sing one of his original songs.

He blinked as if surprised. "Really?"

"Absolutely." Eden nodded enthusiastically. "When?" She immediately regretted asking because it made her seem too eager. Didn't it? She wanted to hear him sing, but only if he wanted to share it. And she didn't want to pin him down to a time. Unless he wanted to be pinned down to a time. *Wow, you are being ridiculous. Hurry and ask him something else.* "What made you go into software?"

Jeremy sat back against the chair, giving Eden an even better view of his toned chest. "I realized that all my playing around on the computer when I was a kid came pretty easy to me, so I went to college and graduated in Software Engineering."

"Jeremy, are you coming back into the hot tub?" Alicia said, interrupting their conversation. She stood there, perfectly posed in her hot pink bikini with her flawless abs.

Jeremy looked up at her. "Sure. I guess." He almost seemed hesitant.

"I have a few emails to catch up on," Eden said, waving her hand and trying to act nonchalant.

He stood. "Come over and join us when you're done." He seemed to be genuinely asking her to join them.

"Oh, yeah, totally," Alicia said, insincerity oozing out.

Alicia was so fake it made Eden want to scream. Instead, Eden smiled and said," I'll be over there soon."

A look of disgust crossed Alicia's face, but she hid it from Jeremy. "Great. See you soon," Alicia said.

Eden snuck a glance at them while they walked over to the far end of the pool. Alicia kept touching him and each time she did, a little shot of irritation zipped through Eden. She reassured herself that the only reason she was bugged was because Alicia had broken into their conversation and that kind of rudeness always bothered Eden. Always. *There is no other reason I'm annoyed.*

Eden finished her fries and sent off an email about little Dylan, whose placement was now in question because his paternal grandmother was demanding he stay with her while Dylan's father was in rehab for the third time.

Eden yawned. Maybe she'd turn in early and get plenty of rest before tomorrow's activities. That seemed to be the best idea because she was tired from traveling.

"Aren't you coming in the pool?" Sophie asked as she walked up to Eden's table.

"I don't think so. I'm going up to the room." She yawned to make her point.

"No way." Sophie held her hands up. "Not yet."

"But—"

"We're going to Tequila Sunrise for some dancing." Sophie shook her hips.

"I don't dance." Some people had rhythm. Some didn't. Eden was the latter.

"You will tonight. I'll even show you how to twerk." Sophie laughed.

"Uh, no thanks. I'm not going to humiliate myself by doing any of that." The last thing Eden wanted to do was twerk. "I'm exhausted from work and then traveling."

"It's my wedding weekend." Sophie made a pouty face. "It won't be the same without you. Besides, you can dance with Jeremy."

Eden inclined her head toward the hot tub. "I think you'd have to ask permission from your cousin." As soon as she said it, she wanted to call it back. It made her sound like some jealous, jilted woman. Which she wasn't.

Sophie shook her head. "Pfft. Don't worry about her. She's a big flirt. And she's a baby. She graduated from high school last year."

"Whatever. I don't care." Except she kind of did, which also irritated her. Why should she care if someone she barely met was in the hot tub with some annoying girl?

"Please, come. It'll be so great. Really." Sophie smiled. "For me?"

Eden knew she was beat. She did come for Sophie and her wedding. The least she could do was hang out with her tonight, even if she'd rather be in her hotel room snuggled under the covers and watching a movie. "For you? Of course."

"Let's go up and change then." Sophie started toward the lobby doors.

Eden followed Sophie up to the room.

"It's like when we were in college," Sophie said as she threw open the door to her room.

"Except we're older and have careers. And you are getting married!"

Sophie jumped up and down. "I am. I am." She clapped her hands. "I can't believe it."

Eden and Sophie hugged.

Sophie stepped into the room and gazed around. "You know, there are too many of us in this room. I'm getting my stuff and moving into your room so we have maximum time together. Is that okay with you?" Sophie said.

"I'd love it."

After they transferred Sophie's stuff to Eden's room, and Sophie texted Antonio to let him know her new room number, Sophie showered. Eden picked out a pink floral print dress from her suitcase. She put it on and examined herself in the large beveled mirror over the dresser.

"Wow, you look stunning in that dress," Sophie said with a towel on her head.

"I bought it for this trip." Eden whirled around.

"Fits you just right and makes your," she paused, "oh, yeah, bronde hair look beautiful."

Eden pulled her hair up on top of her head. "Messy bun?"

"Nah. Leave it down."

They finished getting ready and Eden snatched some perfume to spritz it on her neck.

Sophie inhaled loudly. "Still wearing Victoria's Secret Bombshell?"

"Uh, huh. I love how fruity and floral it is—the perfect combination." Eden finger-styled her hair.

"Remember how that's what got us in trouble when we pranked the girls in our next-door apartment?" Sophie pointed at Eden.

"Oh, yeah. I forgot that little bottle was in the bag. I should've twisted the lid on tighter because when it spilled on that one girl's pillowcase—"

"We were busted."

They both started laughing. Memories washed over Eden reminding her why she loved being with Sophie. "We need to see each other more," Eden said. "I've missed you."

"I know. It's been way too long." Sophie sat on the edge of the bed.

A knock sounded. "Who's that?" Eden asked.

"Probably Antonio. But I'm not ready." Sophie made a face. "Can you tell him to go down to the lobby and wait for me there?"

"Sure."

Sophie popped up from the bed and ducked into the bathroom.

Eden walked over to the door and opened it expecting to see Antonio. Instead, Jeremy stood in the hall.

"Hi," he said while he stood there in faded jeans, a black form-fitting shirt, and a pair of cowboy boots.

Eden drew in a quick breath. "Hi." *What is he doing here? What does he want?*

He looked at Eden, his eyes wide. "Antonio sent me over to tell Sophie he's running a little late."

"So is she." Eden gave an awkward laugh.

"Are you going dancing with us?" His eyes lit up.

She nodded. Dancing was not her forte. When it came to moving to music, Eden didn't know her right foot from her left, but she didn't want Jeremy to know that, especially because he was so musically inclined.

"I guess we'll meet down in the lobby in thirty minutes?" He smiled and the skin around his eyes crinkled.

"Sounds good. I'll tell Sophie." Eden tried to act like it wasn't hard to breathe around him.

"Great. See you then." He dipped his head, then turned around.

Though she wanted to watch him walk away, Eden closed the door and stood there for a moment, her face warm and her chest tingly.

Jeremy was certainly handsome, but she reminded herself that one, she needed to focus on Sophie and the wedding. Two, he didn't seem to mind Alicia falling all over him. And three, she wasn't interested in some weekend fling. Eden smoothed her hair, then went into the bathroom to check on Sophie.

"Your cheeks are all flushed. Are you okay?" Sophie asked.

"I'm fine." Eden wiped at her face.

While Sophie added some mascara she asked, "What did Antonio say?"

"It wasn't Antonio," Eden fluffed her hair.

"Who was it?"

"Jeremy," Eden answered with no inflection in her voice.

"Oh." Sophie stopped applying her mascara and stared at Eden in the mirror.

"What?" Eden's skin felt itchy.

"That's why your face is red." Sophie nodded. "You were talking to Jeremy."

Eden pushed out a breath of indignation at the implication. "That's ridiculous. And totally not true."

"Come on. Admit that you think he's cute." Sophie pointed at her.

Eden was attracted to him, but that didn't mean anything. She was attracted to a lot of men. Not that she could name any others at the moment, but that didn't matter. "You're right, Soph. He's very cute. Gorgeous even. So what?"

Sophie shrugged. "Nothing."

Eden shook her head and walked out into the room to find her sandals.

Chapter Four

Jeremy walked down the hall toward the elevators, his heartbeat thudding in his chest. Eden was so beautiful with her long hair and blue eyes that reminded him of the sky on a summer day. Sophie had talked up her old roommate, but he'd figured Eden wouldn't be that attractive. The few photos he'd seen of her on Instagram certainly didn't do her any justice. But it was more than her beauty that drew him to her.

He pushed the elevator button. *I like the vibe I get from her.* She seemed to be a kind and compassionate person and the way her eyes softened when she spoke of the children tugged at his heart. He hoped he'd be able to spend time with her this weekend and get to know her better. It had been a long time since he'd been this interested in a woman.

The elevator chime dinged and the doors opened. Alicia stood inside. "Oh, hey there, Jeremy. Come on in."

He didn't have much of a choice, so he stepped inside. Immediately, Alicia was at his side, wrapping her arm around his. *She's cute, but way too young for me. And a little annoying.*

"I love country dancing, don't you?" she said as she moved closer to him.

"Sure." He wanted to be polite, but he didn't want to encourage her, especially when his thoughts kept going back to Eden.

"You'll save me plenty of dances, right?" Alicia looked at him, then let her gaze fall to his lips.

He wasn't sure what to say, but before he had to answer the elevator door opened and an older couple entered.

They rode down to the lobby. Alicia was snuggled up to him, making him feel uncomfortable and a little claustrophobic. "Remember, you promised me some dances," she said.

Jeremy gave a slight nod. He was grateful when the doors opened and Alicia left to join some of the other bridesmaids. He wanted to wait for Eden to come down, but didn't know what to do for thirty minutes.

"Jeremy, why don't you come with us?" Alicia said. She walked over to him and invaded his personal space. Again.

What can I tell her? Think of something. "Antonio asked me to wait for him." It wasn't a total lie. Jeremy had offered to wait, so it was close to the truth.

"I'm sure he can find his way over." Alicia ran her fingers along his shoulder. "You can come with us."

"I think I'll wait." He plunged his hands into his pockets.

"Hey, Alicia," said Sydney, one of the other bridesmaids. "We're ready to roll. Are you coming?"

Alicia glanced at Jeremy.

"Go ahead. I'll make sure Sophie and Antonio don't get lost." He laughed.

"I'll look for you when you get there," Alicia said as Sydney tugged on her arm.

Jeremy pasted on a smile. Alicia was pretty with her hazel eyes and dark hair, but he wasn't drawn to her, not like he was to Eden. He looked forward to spending time with Eden tonight.

Chapter Five

Eden finished applying some mascara, then tried to fix her hair. "This is as good as it gets. My hair is going to do whatever it wants tonight."

Sophie wore white capris with sparkles on the back pockets and a fitted rose-colored shirt that complemented her olive skin. "How do I look?" She twirled around.

"Antonio won't be able to take his eyes off you."

Sophie flipped her hair back over her shoulders. "I hope not."

Someone knocked. Sophie opened the door and Antonio stood there alone. For a moment, Eden's heart sank.

"Hey, gorgeous." Antonio took Sophie in his arms and gave her a long kiss. When they came up for air, he said to Eden, "Are you ready for some dancing?"

Eden shrugged. "Sure." She said it as enthusiastically as possible.

"Where's Jeremy?" Sophie asked, then eyed Eden.

"I don't know. Maybe he went over with the rest of the group?" Antonio adjusted the collar on his blue shirt.

Eden let her mind wander. She imagined Jeremy already dancing with Alicia, her arms draped all over him, and the both of them laughing and enjoying themselves together. A tinge of something raced down her back. She didn't want to interpret it, because in the end it didn't matter. They were here for a few days and that was it.

They took the elevator down to the lobby and when the doors opened, Eden immediately spotted Jeremy. Her heartbeat echoed in her ears and heat crept up her neck.

"Jeremy," Sophie shouted, waving her arm.

He looked over and when his gaze met Eden's, a smile spread across his face. He walked over to them.

"I thought you'd gone with the others," Antonio said.

"I wanted to wait for you and Sophie to make sure you didn't get lost on your way over." He grinned.

"That's not a bad idea." Antonio started kissing Sophie on her neck.

Sophie laughed, then swatted at him. "Come on. We need to meet everyone."

Inside Antonio's white Jeep Wrangler, Eden and Jeremy sat in the back. A faint, sweet, earthy scent that reminded Eden of the outdoors floated in the air.

"Do you do much country dancing?" Jeremy asked.

Trying not to choke on her reply, Eden said, "Not a lot." *Make that not even a little bit.*

"Eden was the studious one in college. She graduated Summa Cum Laude," Sophie said.

Eden's face warmed. "I like to learn."

"Not much for the party scene in college?" Jeremy said.

"I wanted to get good grades and be able to graduate as soon as possible." She crossed her ankles and tried to relax.

"I made her stop studying every once in a while and live a little," Sophie said.

"Living a little by her definition was living on the edge," Eden said as she nodded.

Sophie started laughing. "College was amazing. And Austin is so beautiful. And quirky. And awesome."

"Great memories," Eden said. "And I have Sophie to thank for making me get out and live a little." She laughed.

When they arrived in the parking lot and stopped the car, Jeremy turned to Eden and said, "Wait a sec."

Puzzled, Eden sat in her seat. The next thing she knew, Jeremy was opening her door. *What a gentleman. Most men don't do this.* He extended his hand and she willingly placed hers in his. A pins and needles sensation traveled up her arm. He then shut her door and stood next to her side.

Sophie winked at her as if to say, *this is a good one.*

"Thank you," Eden said.

"My nana taught me to always open doors for women." Jeremy smiled and it made Eden's stomach somersault.

Handsome, polite, and respectful. I wouldn't mind spending some more time with him.

They walked into Tequila Sunrise, the lively music ringing through the air. Antonio excused himself to use the restroom.

"Looks like we found the right place," Sophie said as she waved to the wedding party.

Alicia rushed over. She eyed Eden up and down, making it obvious she wasn't pleased Jeremy had come with her. "Hey, we're getting started. Do you want to dance?" She held her hand out for Jeremy.

"Uh," he glanced at Eden. "Sure."

Alicia pulled him out to the dance floor.

Sophie leaned over and said, "I'm going to have a talk with her."

"About what?" Eden asked.

"About how she's acting with Jeremy." Sophie frowned.

"Why?" Eden didn't want this to turn into some drama.

Sophie looked at her. "Because he's not interested in my cousin."

Eden watched them together. She tamped down a flare of jealousy, then said, "Looks like they're having fun."

"I think he wants more than fun." Sophie leaned in closer. "He told Antonio he wished he could find a good woman and settle down, but he hasn't met anyone like that yet."

"I'm not sure why you're telling me this." Eden blinked.

Sophie rolled her eyes.

Eden pointed at herself. "I'm not interested in a relationship."

"Why not?" Sophie raised her eyebrows.

How could she explain it? "Not only am I super busy with my job, but even if I had time for a relationship, I've seen way too much heartbreak. Over and over again. I'm not sure I even believe in marriage and all that anymore." She touched Sophie on the arm. "You and Antonio are the exception. Not the rule."

Sophie knit her brows together. "You don't want to get married and have kids?"

"Soph, I'm here to celebrate your wedding. Not to find a man."

"But—"

"Really. Stop worrying about me and focus on your handsome groom." Eden inclined her head. "Here he comes."

"How about a dance?" Antonio said. He wrapped his arms around Sophie.

"I'd love to, but . . ." She glanced at Eden.

"Don't worry about me. Go celebrate."

Eden found a table and sat so she could watch Sophie and Antonio dance. They were a perfect match. An anomaly. Even putting aside her experience with broken families, other than Sophie, most of Eden's girlfriends weren't finding decent men. Her co-workers complained about bad relationships and men who cheated and lied. Eden avoided all of that by not becoming involved with anyone. Besides, the kids needed her full attention. She didn't want to waste time on a man. Not even a man as attractive as Jeremy.

"Can I get you something to drink?" a waitress with a cowboy hat and a short denim skirt asked.

"I'm good, thanks."

The waitress walked away. Eden drummed her fingers on the table while a song about the sun going down played. Antonio and Sophie danced all over the dance floor. Sophie laughed as they made their way around. Sophie looked beautiful and so happy, which made Eden's heart happy as well.

Eden casually scanned the dance floor but didn't see Jeremy or Alicia. *They must be outside together. They're probably a much better match than Sophie thinks.*

"Is this seat taken?" came a deep voice behind her. Eden turned to see Jeremy.

She shook her head. *Where is your tag-along?* "Tired of dancing?"

"I guess that depends on the partner." He smiled.

What's that supposed to mean? He wants a different one? He doesn't want to dance with Alicia?

"How about you come and dance a few with me?" He sat next to her.

"I'm not much of a dancer." She could think of one thousand things she'd rather do than dance, including having a root canal.

"You might enjoy it." He cupped his hand around his mouth and whispered, "I think it'd make Sophie happy to see you out there."

No matter how much she wanted to, she couldn't argue with that. It wouldn't last too long, and there was a big crowd that she could blend into. Maybe it wouldn't be so bad, after all. "You win. But you might have to teach me a few steps."

As they got out to the dance floor, the DJ announced it was time for a line dance. Although she'd heard of line dancing, Eden had never done it. *I need to get out more.* She gave Jeremy a help-me-figure-out-how-to-do-this look.

Picking up on her hesitation, Jeremy said, "Don't worry. It's pretty easy. Follow me."

Jeremy stepped to the right, kicked his right foot, tapped his foot, kicked again, then stepped to the left and swiveled his hips. Eden tried to do the same but stepped right when she was supposed to step left, and ended on the wrong foot. She didn't even attempt to swivel anything.

Jeremy showed her again. Eden drew in a breath and tried it, but this time kicked when she should've stepped.

She could tell Jeremy was trying to stifle a laugh at the uncoordinated mess she called a body. "Sorry, I'm so bad at this."

Jeremy stepped behind her and placed his hands on her hips, creating hot spots on either side of her. He leaned in to tell her, "I'll guide you this time." She tried not to notice how close he was behind her or how his warm breath on her neck made goosebumps erupt along her neck.

He gently guided her to the right and said, "Now kick, tap, kick again." He gave her some pressure to move to the left. When it came time to swivel her hips, Jeremy softly pushed her from one side to the other. "You got it," he said with enthusiasm.

Eden said over her shoulder, "Watch out, I'm ready for *Dancing with the Stars*."

Jeremy started laughing, so she turned around and playfully slapped at his arm.

He held his hands up. "Sorry. I didn't mean to—"

"Not all of us have moves like you," she said. Jeremy seemed so comfortable on the dance floor.

He lifted his eyebrow slightly, then smiled. "Let's try it again."

They spent the rest of the song line dancing. And by the end, Eden wasn't awful. She wasn't good, but she didn't look like a full body dry heave.

"See, you got the hang of it." He nodded.

"Thanks for teaching me. I'll remember it when I never line dance again." She laughed.

The music slowed and Jeremy said, "'Wanted' by Hunter Hayes."

"Huh?" Eden looked at Jeremy.

"The name of the song is 'Wanted' and it's sung by Hunter Hayes."

"Oh. Got it." Eden hadn't ever wished she knew more about country songs until tonight.

Jeremy offered his hand and Eden accepted. He pulled her close to him, her cheek touching his and making the nerves along her neck fire rapidly. She let herself sink into his strong, capable arms noting how comfortable she felt there. Eden listened to the words of the song as they moved in tempo to the music and found herself wondering what it would be like to be wrapped up in his embrace and kissing his lips. She closed her eyes, imagining it when suddenly someone tapped her on the shoulder. Blinking, she stepped back.

"I think Sophie might need you," Alicia said with a distressed look on her face.

Eden glanced around. She didn't see Sophie on the dance floor. "Why? What happened?"

"I don't know for sure, but she was out in the parking lot and she seemed upset." Alicia sounded concerned.

"Oh." Eden stepped back. "I should go find her."

Jeremy dropped his hands and said, "I can come with you."

"I'm not sure that's a good idea," Alicia said. "I think it's a girl thing."

"I'll see you later," Eden said.

Eden normally would've been irritated at the interruption, but she was worried about Sophie. She hurried out the door to the parking lot, playing scenarios in her mind as she searched for Sophie. *I hope she's okay.* She walked to her left and scanned the area, then turned to her right to see if she could locate Sophie. Her best friend was nowhere to be seen. *I hope this isn't about the wedding.*

Eden traveled around the back of the building, her heart beating fast, but didn't see Sophie there either. *Where is she? What's going on?*

Eden pulled out her phone and called Sophie.

"Hey," Sophie said when she answered the phone.

"Where are you?" Eden asked, trying to remain calm.

Sophie giggled. "Antonio wanted some alone time, so we took a walk along the beach. I'm sorry we left. Is everything okay?"

"I was wondering where you were. That's all." She balled her fist. "Have you seen Alicia?"

"Oh, yeah. We ran into her on our way out to the beach. She was going back inside Tequila's." Sophie sounded fine. Better than fine.

"Thanks."

"Are you looking for her?"

Eden tried to mask her anger because she didn't want to upset Sophie. "I just needed to talk to her about something. No biggie. Go back to your alone time. I'll talk to you later." Eden ended the call, then let out a loud sigh.

She was glad that Sophie was okay, but, apparently, Alicia wanted Jeremy to herself and had to resort to trickery to get rid of Eden. *How childish and immature.*

Eden marched back into Tequila's ready to give Alicia a piece of her mind, but stopped in her tracks. On the dance floor, Alicia was hanging all over Jeremy and he didn't seem to mind it. *Wait. What am I doing?* Eden laughed to herself. No matter how she'd felt while she danced with Jeremy, obviously it was one-sided. If he wanted to dance with Alicia all night long, then he was welcome to it. She didn't have time for such nonsense.

Eden searched for a cab company on her phone. When she found one, she called to get a ride back to the hotel. On the drive over, she refused to let herself think about the situation, because it wasn't worth it. Instead, she mindlessly surfed through Instagram until they arrived at the hotel.

When she got to her room, she collapsed on the bed. She still didn't want to think about Jeremy. Or their easy conversation. Or the dance lessons. Or feeling his arms around her as they swayed to the music on the dance floor. She rolled to her side and clenched her jaw. Sure, she'd enjoyed dancing with Jeremy, maybe even felt a little something for him as he held her, but she wasn't about to play games with Alicia. She was only here for the weekend and there was no reason whatsoever to get involved in this silly competition with another bridesmaid. Alicia was welcome to all of Jeremy's attention.

Because Eden didn't care.

At all.

Chapter Six

Jeremy sat at a table alongside a window, then leaned back in the chair. He'd been dancing with some of the bridesmaids while he waited for Eden to return. He again scanned the room, but she was nowhere in sight. *I hope she's coming back.*

Alicia approached the table wearing a wide smile. "Come out and dance with me again." She held out her hand expectantly.

Jeremy shook his head. "I think I'm going to sit out for a while." He wasn't used to so much dancing and his feet were beginning to hurt. Back in Dallas, he spent any free time he had writing songs or playing one of his instruments.

Alicia set her hands on her hips and gave him a pout. "But I need another dance with you," she said in an abnormally soft voice.

He'd already had enough dancing with Alicia for the night—maybe even for the duration. *Where is Eden? If only she would show up right now.* "You've worn me out, Alicia." He hoped that'd be enough of a hint for her.

"All right. You rest for a bit. But I'll be back." She winked at him, then turned and sashayed away. Jeremy laughed to himself. Alicia was certainly amusing.

He continued to scan Tequila's. He thought about going outside, but he didn't want to barge in on anything with Eden and Sophie. He couldn't imagine that Sophie or Antonio would be having cold feet. They were the most well-matched couple he'd met, and they'd been planning this wedding for over a year. *Must be something else.*

Jeremy stood to go find the restroom when he saw Sophie and Antonio walk inside. He made his way over to them. "Is everything okay?" he asked.

"Sure." Sophie smiled. "Why?"

"Alicia told Eden you needed help or something." He checked his watch. "That was over thirty minutes ago."

"That's weird. Eden called to check on me, but I told her everything was fine. We did see Alicia earlier after I'd stubbed my toe. She must've thought I needed more help, I guess." Sophie shrugged.

"Eden never came back."

Sophie glanced around. "She didn't?"

Jeremy shook his head. "No." He knew, because he'd been watching for her ever since she left.

"I bet she went to the hotel." Sophie nodded. "She was pretty tired. That girl works all the time. Never takes a break." Sophie held up her hand. "I bet she's sound asleep by now."

Jeremy tried to hide his disappointment. He'd looked forward to spending more time with Eden, but she'd disappeared. He couldn't quite get a read on her.

"Hey, handsome, are you ready for another dance now?" Alicia said.

Alicia, on the other hand, was easy to read. "I think I'm going to call it a night." No one else held his interest enough for him to stay any longer.

Alicia wrinkled her nose and gave him an indignant look. "It's way too early to go back to the hotel."

"I think we'll head back as well," Sophie said. "I need my beauty sleep."

"Not you, baby. No amount of sleep could make you any more beautiful." Antonio smiled.

Jeremy shook his head. "You two."

"Hey, man, when you find your true love, you'll be just like us."

Antonio pointed at Jeremy, then he and Sophie started walking toward the door.

Jeremy shrugged. Would he find a love like Antonio had with Sophie? He wasn't sure. But if he ever did, he'd hang onto it, because it seemed to be a rarity.

He glanced over at Alicia, who was staring at him. "I think I'll catch a ride with the lovebirds."

"Oh, no. Please, stay," Alicia pleaded. "I promise you won't regret it." She moved in close to him.

"Thanks, but I'll see you in the morning." He didn't want to be rude to Sophie's cousin, but she didn't seem to pick up on the fact that he wasn't really interested in her. Hopefully, she'd find another guy to keep her occupied.

"I can't wait to see you tomorrow morning." She leaned in and kissed him on the cheek before he could react.

Jeremy wasn't sure what to say, so he dipped his head and left.

Chapter Seven

The following morning, Eden awoke to the blow dryer. She wiped the sleep from her eyes and pushed her tangled hair from her face. She must've fallen asleep as soon as her head hit the pillow.

"Hey," she said to Sophie in the bathroom.

Sophie shut off the blow dryer and stood there with half-wet hair, "What happened to you last night?"

"I was tired, so I decided to come back here." It was completely true. She was tired. And she was tired of Alicia.

Sophie pointed her brush at Eden. "Jeremy was looking all over for you."

"I bet." She was certain Jeremy didn't have time to look for her when he was dancing it up with Alicia.

"What?" Sophie looked at Eden with a puzzled expression.

"Nothing." It wasn't worth it to say anything to Sophie and get pulled into some silly drama with a teenager over a guy she'd barely met. Eden ran her fingers through her hair, then pulled it into a ponytail using a rubber band from around her wrist. "What's on the agenda for today?"

"We have a full day planned." Sophie's whole face beamed. "We're going on a boat to watch for dolphins, then horseback riding on the beach, and then we'll do a wedding rehearsal and dinner. It's going to be amazing!"

Eden didn't care much for horses, but watching dolphins sounded interesting. And she wanted to support Sophie. "It'll be awesome. Except I'm not really a horse person, you know."

"Don't worry about that. These horses are super gentle."

"I'm excited." She wasn't, but she didn't have the heart to spoil Sophie's big day. Not only was Eden not into animals, she didn't particularly want to spend time with Jeremy and, even more, she definitely didn't want to be stuck all day with Alicia. Was there any way for her to ditch the day? Probably not. She'd have to suck it up and be the best maid of honor possible for Sophie, because at the end of the day, Sophie's happiness trumped everything else.

After they got ready, Sophie and Eden went down to the restaurant to meet everyone for breakfast. Eden tensed the closer she got to the restaurant.

"There's my handsome fiancé." Sophie squealed and ran to meet Antonio, leaving Eden awkwardly alone.

"There you are," came a voice from behind her. Eden whirled around to see Jeremy. He looked quite handsome in his plaid shorts and fitted light blue v-neck t-shirt. She almost forgot that she wasn't interested in talking to him anymore. "Where did you go last night?" he asked.

"Oh, uh." What could she say? *I left because Alicia is a snake and successfully sent me outside. When I came in, you didn't look like you missed me at all.* That sounded completely pathetic. And she wasn't pathetic.

Jeremy gazed at her with his chocolatey brown eyes. "And?"

"I went out to check on Sophie. When I didn't find her," she paused. *This is my chance. I can tell him what Alicia did.*

"Go on," he said, waiting.

There was no problem with Sophie. Alicia maneuvered me out of the room so she could dance with you, and you looked like you enjoyed it. Which is totally fine with me. "I called her and everything seemed to be fine. I realized how exhausted I was, so I went back to the hotel."

He studied her. She didn't want to melt under his gaze, so she moved over to the table.

"We're going to have breakfast and then it's off to Dolphin Adventures for our boat ride. I hope you're all ready." Sophie clapped her hands together. Excitement oozed out of her and it was hard to not share her enthusiasm.

Eden gave herself a pep talk. It didn't matter that Alicia did her dirty last night. This weekend wasn't about anyone else but Sophie. *I need to relax and enjoy myself with my best friend.*

Eden sat at the long table and Jeremy took a seat next to her.

"Good morning, everybody," Alicia said as she came gliding into the room. "I'm starving." She glanced around the room and her gaze settled on Jeremy. She sat on the other side of him.

Remember, this weekend is about Sophie, not her devious cousin. Eden sipped ice cold water and focused on Sophie.

"I hear we're going horseback riding later today," Jeremy said as he turned to Eden, a whiff of his cologne wafting past her.

Have a casual, normal conversation with him. "That's what Sophie said. She's got the whole day planned."

"Have you ridden horses before?"

"No. Have you?" she asked flippantly, certain that Jeremy was a city boy and hadn't been around horses either.

"Actually, I grew up on a ranch in Montana." He gave her a slight smile as if he thought his answer would surprise her.

She blinked, then cleared her throat. "A ranch? Like with cows and horses?"

"Yes ma'am."

This is unexpected. He seems like such an urbanite. "So, you're a cowboy?"

He nodded. "I don't have much need to wear my cowboy hat to work anymore, but I used to help my grandpa and my dad with the cattle. And I used to milk Lana."

"Lana?"

"Our Holstein."

Eden stared at him. *What is a Holstein?*

He watched her for a moment, picking up on her confusion he said, "Our cow."

"Oh." She blinked. This guy wasn't anything like she'd figured. "You milked a cow? And named it Lana?"

He nodded. "You know, after Lana Lang from *Smallville*." He sounded so matter-of-factly.

"You named your cow after a character in a TV show?" She bit her lip to prevent a laugh from falling out.

"Oh, yeah. All my friends had crushes on her. She was the topic of many conversations back in the day."

"And to honor her, you named your cow after her?"

He scratched his head. "It made sense to my teenage mind at the time."

She couldn't help but smile at the absurdity of naming a cow after a TV show character. "What else did you do on the ranch?" She found herself fascinated with this man.

"I collected fresh eggs in the morning before school."

"Did you name all the chickens? And the eggs?" She laughed.

"Nah. Too many of them. But we did name the rooster."

"I can't even imagine." She'd never met anyone like Jeremy before. "What was the rooster's name?"

"Solomon."

She knew the answer to this one. "Because he had like seven hundred wives?" she said proudly.

"I'm impressed."

"I went to Bible camp and we learned all about Solomon." She recalled lessons about many of the Bible characters.

Jeremy nodded with a pleased expression.

Eden leaned in, smiling to herself that she'd had his uninterrupted attention. "Why did you leave the ranch?"

A pained expression flashed across Jeremy's face. "We fell on hard times. Grandpa sold off his portion and my dad ended up with only a few acres. Grandpa retired. My dad works in town and my mom teaches school, so there's not much for me there now."

"Excuse me?" Alicia said in an ear-splitting voice, breaking into their conversation. "Can you please pass the water pitcher?"

Eden picked up the pitcher and handed it to Alicia, who gave her an insincere smile.

The slim waitress with salt-and-pepper hair said, "Y'all are welcome to get your breakfast at the buffet bar. Please use a clean plate every time. And let me know if ya need anything at all."

Both Eden and Jeremy stood and walked over to the buffet. Eden spooned some fruit onto her plate.

"I love pancakes," Alicia said behind them. "My favorite breakfast food." She piled some on her plate then drowned them with syrup.

Eden wasn't at all interested in what Alicia liked to eat for breakfast.

Jeremy filled his plate with eggs, hash browns, bacon, and a biscuit. He followed Eden back to the table and they sat down.

"Where did you grow up?" he asked.

"My dad works for an oil company so we spent time overseas when I was young, then moved to Houston when I was about ten. I graduated from high school and went over to Austin for college. That's where I met Sophie."

"Where overseas?" He bit into a piece of bacon.

"Saudi mostly." Eden took a sip of water. "It was a very different culture and lifestyle, that's for sure."

"Do you miss it?"

"Excuse me," Alicia said as she began maneuvering behind them to get to her seat.

Eden mentally rolled her eyes. This girl was so obvious. And so obnoxious. Without warning, a noise sounded behind her and Eden felt a warm gooey substance hit her neck.

"Oh my. I am so sorry," Alicia said. "I've spilled my food on you."

Eden felt the back of her head only to discover sticky syrup all in her hair.

"I'll get you some napkins," Alicia offered.

Anger bubbled inside Eden. No one would blame her if she told Alicia where to go. Alicia more than deserved it, because this was no accident. Just another one of Alicia's little antics to get Jeremy's attention. *I'd like to strangle her right here.* Eden sucked in a deep breath while all eyes were on her. The last thing she wanted to do was create some big scene and lower herself to Alicia's level. "I think I'll need to take a shower, actually." Obviously, that was Alicia's plan.

Sophie came rushing over. "Alicia, what is wrong with you? Look what you've done."

"It was an accident. I didn't mean to spill it on her." Alicia sounded stunned that anyone would even think that.

"You are ruining this breakfast." Sophie pointed at her watch. "We have reservations and now we'll be late."

Eden held her hand up. "No, no. Eat breakfast and go on to the activity. I'll take a shower and catch up with you."

"It won't be the same without you. I want you there," Sophie said with a crestfallen expression. "This is all your fault, Alicia."

Eden was tempted to let Sophie yell at Alicia more, but decided to intercede to keep Sophie calm. "It's not a big deal, really, Soph. I'll meet you over there."

Sophie's shoulders slumped. "I guess so. But don't take too long."

"I promise to hurry," Eden said, proud of herself for staying calm even though she wanted to give Alicia a thorough tongue-lashing.

"I am so sorry," Alicia said with as much sincerity as a politician during an election.

Eden gave her an I-don't-believe-you-at-all smile. She made her way back to her room with her sticky, maple-scented hair.

After she removed her tainted shirt, Eden put it in the sink, then quickly disrobed so she didn't get the syrup on any other clothing. Inside the steaming shower, Eden had to laugh. Was Alicia so desperate for a man she had to resort to tricks? In a way, Eden felt sorry for her. *Alicia must not feel very confident in her own ability to attract a good guy like Jeremy.*

Eden lathered up the shampoo, her thoughts centering on Jeremy. She was still shocked that he was a cowboy, but it wasn't difficult to imagine him wearing a cowboy hat and fitted jeans with a t-shirt that hugged him in all the right places while his muscles flexed as he lifted hay bales. What a sight that would be to see Jeremy riding a horse and working with cows.

Eden let out a long breath. Too bad she'd met him under these circumstances when another woman—who acted more like a lovesick teenager—had set her sights on him and obviously meant to make Eden miserable in the process.

While she'd like to get to know Jeremy, Eden wasn't at all interested in some kind of feud with Sophie's immature cousin, especially because in a few days they'd all go back to their real lives.

Eden finished her shower and wrapped her hair in a towel. It had only taken four times to wash the gummy mess out. She went to her suitcase and found a pair of skinny jeans and white blouse. She blow-dried her hair and reapplied her mascara and eye liner, then found some hoop earrings and a silver bracelet. Eden was ready to go to Dolphin Adventure. She found it on her phone and was about to call for a cab when someone knocked at

her door.

Chapter Eight

Eden opened the door to Jeremy.

"Hi," he said.

Eden swallowed hard. "Uh, hi. I didn't expect to see you here."

"I hope you don't mind. I told Sophie you'd need a ride over there and volunteered to wait for you." He smiled and Eden was sure his smile could illuminate a small city.

"Thanks." She was touched by his thoughtfulness, but feared what Alicia would do next. Eden did not want to be in the middle of anything. Girl drama was not her thing.

"I thought you might be ready." He slipped his hands in his pockets.

Holding up her phone, Eden said, "I was about to call for a taxi."

"Now you won't need one."

Eden stuck her phone in the back pocket of her jeans and stepped outside the room, closing the door behind her. "I don't know if we'll make the boat ride or not."

Jeremy motioned for her to walk toward the elevator. "If not, there's a sea life center where we can wait for the group."

They chatted inside the elevator as they rode it down to the lobby. They walked outside to the car and Eden halfway expected Alicia to pop out at any minute and do something else to her. She was relieved when they reached the car and Alicia was nowhere in sight.

Jeremy opened the door to a black Toyota Camry for her and she slid across the seat. Watching him as he walked around the front of the car, Eden found herself fascinated by such a good-looking, respectful and polite man. She didn't meet many men like Jeremy. Though Alicia was annoying and sneaky rude, she couldn't blame her for being captivated by Jeremy as well.

They drove over to the dolphin center, chatting easily about music and a couple of movies they'd both seen and enjoyed.

"Here it is," Jeremy said. He pulled the car into a parking lot. A large blue sign welcomed them to the Dolphin and Ocean Life Adventure Center.

They walked inside the immense space and over to a reception desk. Jeremy said, "We're with a group for the dolphin cruise."

"It's a wedding party," Eden said. "Sophie and Antonio."

"Oh, I'm so sorry," the middle- aged woman with short brown hair said. "We held the cruise for as long as we could, but we had to stay on schedule. I'm sorry."

Eden's shoulders fell. She knew Sophie must've left disappointed that Eden and Jeremy hadn't made it there in time to go on the cruise. And all because Alicia purposely drenched Eden in syrup.

"We have a lot to do here while you wait. You can pet the manta rays, meet Oscar our turtle, watch us feed the sea horses, and look at all our different aquariums. We also have information about dolphins. I can make you a reservation on the next cruise if you'd like," the woman said brightly.

"Thank you. I don't think we'll make reservations right now. We'll wait for everyone to get back," Jeremy said.

They walked toward one of the exhibits. "I feel so bad. I know Sophie is sad." Eden didn't want anything to dampen Sophie's spirits this weekend.

"It wasn't your fault." Jeremy shook his head and a lock of his thick hair fell across his forehead.

No, it was Alicia's. "I didn't mean to make you miss the dolphin cruise too."

Jeremy flashed a quick smile. "Can I be honest?"

"Sure." *What is he going to say? That Alicia is a rude, childish woman and he's glad he doesn't have to be around her?* Eden waited for his enlightened response.

"I get a little seasick, so this was a good excuse for me." He seemed a little embarrassed by his admission.

"Oh." Not what she expected him to say.

He peered at her and it made her heart clamp tight. "And," he paused, "it worked out well for us to spend some time together." He stepped closer to her.

A smile worked around the edges of her mouth. *He wants to spend time with me.* Warmth enveloped her. Alicia's plan may have been executed well, but it might have just backfired on her. At least Eden hoped it had backfired.

"Would you like to pet the mantas?" Jeremy asked.

"I'd love to," she said. Petting a slimy sea creature wasn't high on her list of priorities, but if it meant spending time with Jeremy, she was all for it.

They made their way over to a large open-topped tank where several manta rays swam. They looked so graceful as they slid through the water using their large fins. As one swam past, Jeremy stuck his hand into the water, so Eden followed suit. The water was cool and as the fish swam by, it felt smooth and squishy.

"They're related to sharks. They don't breathe air. They have gills so they can respire water." He sounded so authoritative.

"Wow. You know a lot about these animals." She was impressed with his knowledge of sea life.

Jeremy pointed to a sign behind Eden. "Actually, I'm a great reader." He laughed.

They watched the triangular-looking fish swim through the tank. It was almost mesmerizing to see them glide through the water.

"We'll be feeding the seahorses in Seahorse Cove," a woman's voice announced over the speaker.

"Let's watch that," Eden said. "I've always been fascinated by seahorses. I love the way they look and how they propel themselves in the water. If I had an aquarium, I'd want to have it filled with seahorses. Did you know that the males carry the babies?"

"Interesting. I think I'm glad I'm not a seahorse." He patted his stomach.

Eden laughed. "I did a huge project on seahorses for my marine biology class back in high school. I loved that class. I even thought about being a marine biologist for a hot second after I took that class."

When they arrived at the Seahorse Cove they stood near a large aquarium. Eden spotted two seahorses with their tails intertwined.

"They must like each other," Jeremy said as he edged closer to the glass.

Eden moved near him and stared at the seahorses. "I think you're right."

Jeremy slipped his hand into Eden's. She liked how his hand felt in hers. Strong, but gentle, soft, and so natural—like her hand belonged in his.

They stood, hand in hand, for a few minutes watching the seahorse couple swim around the tank. Eden could've stayed there all day with him. A tingle of excitement ran down her back.

"Should we go meet Oscar?" Jeremy said.

"Yeah." At that moment, Eden would've gone to meet anyone, or anything, as long as she was with Jeremy.

"I used to have a turtle when I was a kid." He laughed. "One time I had the turtle out in the yard and one of our cats got too close. The turtle snapped and actually grabbed onto the cat's face."

Eden gasped. "Oh no. Did it hurt the cat?" She covered her mouth.

"He ran all over the yard with the turtle attached. We tried to help, but Bruce wouldn't let us. The turtle finally let go. Both of them were fine." Jeremy held up a finger. "Bruce never got close to my turtle again."

"You named your cat Bruce?" She suppressed a smile.

"Yep, Bruce Wayne." Jeremy nodded proudly.

"You're also a Batman fan?"

"Of course." He shrugged. "I read all the comic books. Batman is the coolest superhero."

"So, you're a computer nerd *and* a superhero fan?" Sounded like the perfect combination to her.

He tipped his head. "Guilty as charged."

Jeremy was the most intriguing man Eden had met in a long time. An incredibly handsome cowboy who named a cow after a TV character, loved comic books, worked on computers, and was kind and thoughtful.

When they got to another tank, a big sign hung over it with the name Oscar in fancy letters. A large sea turtle swam around.

"He reminds me of that turtle on *Finding Nemo*," Eden said.

Jeremy half closed his eyes and bobbed his head. "So, like, whoa dude, my name is Crush."

Eden started laughing at his impersonation of one of her favorite characters. "That's very good. Maybe you should go into voice overs for Disney movies if your career in computers ever ends."

"You think so, dude?" he said, still in character.

"Like totally," Eden said.

They both started laughing. Eden hadn't had this much fun in a long time. It wasn't technically a date, but she hadn't spent time with a man that made her feel so light and happy in forever.

They continued to look at the different tanks and talk about the sea life contained in the tanks. While they were admiring the starfish, the wedding party walked into the center.

Sophie rushed over. "Eden, I missed you!"

"I know. I'm so sorry. When we got here, you guys had already left."

Sophie looked between Jeremy and Eden, then her gaze landed on their still interlocked hands. A grin splashed across her face. "It's fine. Don't even worry about it."

"How was the cruise?" Eden asked, trying to act as if it were completely natural to be holding Jeremy's hand.

"We saw so many dolphins. Some of them even jumped out of the water. It was so cool." She held her hands up.

"Where is everyone else?" *Specifically, where is Alicia?* Eden wasn't sure how Sophie's cousin would react when she saw Eden and Jeremy holding hands. Would Alicia push her into a tank or something?

"Poor Alicia, she got so sick on the boat she had to go back to the hotel to rest. A couple of girls went with her." Sophie clutched at her chest.

"That's too bad," Eden said, hoping she didn't sound as insincere as she felt.

"She actually barfed over the side of the boat," Sophie whispered. "I was embarrassed for her."

Eden didn't want to say that karma had come to kick Alicia in the behind, so she simply smiled to herself. A great big smile.

The rest of the wedding party joined them and they spent time exploring the center. Eden enjoyed learning how to be a better caretaker of the ocean, but mostly she enjoyed walking around holding hands with Jeremy.

Sophie glanced at her watch. "It's time to go to Adventure World and ride horses."

"I'm a little nervous to ride a horse," Eden said. "I've never been on one before, and I'm petrified it'll run away with me."

Sophie waved her hand. "Don't worry. They assured me that the horses are very gentle and they'll only walk. It's going to be super fun."

Eden wasn't sure she'd call riding a horse *fun*. They were huge animals with enormous strength. And she was about to trust her life with one.

"Don't worry. I'll be riding right next to you," Jeremy said with a smile that reassured her.

On the drive over, Jeremy and Eden chatted about the Superbowl and how the Cowboys would definitely be in the next one.

"I hope Alicia makes it over to horseback riding," Sophie said from the backseat.

I hope she doesn't. Eden didn't want to be a terrible person, but she was enjoying her time with Jeremy and didn't want Alicia to ruin it.

"I'm sure she'll be there," Antonio said.

"I just want everything to be perfect this weekend," Sophie said.

Eden's heart softened toward Alicia, because she wanted Sophie to have the weekend of her dreams, but she still wasn't going to cry if Alicia didn't make it.

They drove along a road that followed the Gulf until they found Adventure Park.

"Oh, here it is," Sophie said with excitement. "This is going to be so awesome!"

Antonio and Jeremy both jumped out of the car and opened the doors. Jeremy held out his hand for Eden and she willingly took it.

Most of the others in the wedding party were congregated at the stables. Eden quickly scanned the group and was pleased that Alicia wasn't among them.

Gabriella, one of the bridesmaids, twisted her long black hair into a bun and secured it on her head with a clip. "I love riding horses. Sophie, remember when we used to go to Abuela's house and ride the horses? Alicia was always taking extra turns when we'd go."

"And that time she fell off in the corral and landed in the manure?" Sophie said.

Eden started laughing at the thought of Alicia with a face full of manure.

Sophie and Gabriella both looked at Eden, and she realized she'd laughed too much and too loud. Eden cleared her throat and said, "So, we're going to ride them on the beach?"

"Yes," Sophie said.

Antonio walked over to the guide and said, "I want the best horse for my bride-to-be because she deserves the best."

Eden let out a breath of envy, wishing she'd find someone like Antonio someday—someone who'd think she deserved the best.

"We'll put her on Midnight," said the man with a bushy moustache and a worn cowboy hat.

"I'm here," Alicia's grate-on-your-nerves-voice rang out.

Eden watched her rush over to the group with a couple of the other bridesmaids. Alicia hugged Sophie and said, "I'm so sorry I got sick, but I feel much better now."

"I'm glad you made it."

"I'd like the most gentle," Eden said, twisting her silver bracelet around her wrist. "I've never ridden a horse before."

"Yes, ma'am. Patches over here is a good one for you." He said it in a way to comfort her, but Eden didn't feel too confident. She wanted to get this ride over with.

The man with the cowboy hat helped Eden up onto the dark brown horse with a black mane. Trying to keep her heartbeat steady, she said, "Thanks. Do I steer him with these?" She held up the reins. Snickering sounded, but she wasn't sure where it came from.

The man nodded with a grin. "Yes, ma'am that's how you *steer* the horse."

What had she said wrong? Her question seemed legitimate to her. Wouldn't you steer a horse like you steer a car?

The horse took a few steps. "Okay, horse, let's take it easy," Eden said, wishing she'd skipped this part of the activities.

Jeremy rode up next to her. "The key to enjoying a ride is to relax," he said, looking quite natural in the saddle.

"That's easy for you to say. You're like a cowboy person. I'm not." Eden was becoming increasingly anxious about the ride.

"I'll ride next to you the whole way." His voice was calm and soothing.

Eden gave a tight smile. "That'd make me feel better." *In more ways than one.*

"Hey, everyone," Antonio said. "We're going to follow a trail out to the beach. Ernie here will go with us." He pointed at the man with the moustache.

Eden shifted her weight in the saddle. Maybe if she relaxed it'd all be over sooner. *People have been riding horses for centuries, certainly I can do it for an hour or so.* Jeremy let her go in front of him. Patches seemed to fall into line behind the other horses, which made Eden feel a tad bit more comfortable on this gigantic beast.

They all followed a path out to the sand. The sun was beginning to descend, but the air was still warm and moist, especially for a February day. Eden had been out of Texas weather long enough to grow an affinity for Portland's cooler temperatures.

When they got to the beach area, the horses spread out, so Jeremy rode up alongside her. "See, nothing to it."

"Maybe." She still wasn't convinced.

Jeremy smoothed his hair. "I used to ride a horse all over the ranch in Montana. I don't get much of a chance in Dallas."

Starting to relax, Eden loosened her grip on the reins. "It's nice being out here on the beach."

"It's peaceful being on a horse enjoying the sounds of nature," he said.

The sand stretched out before them and the waves lapped against the shore in a tranquil, melodic rhythm. *Maybe this isn't so bad.*

"Grandpa used to say if you had some thinking to do, get on a horse and ride out to a solitary place where you could clear your mind." Jeremy fanned his hand out.

"Sounds like good advice."

A commotion sounded behind them, but Eden was too scared to turn around. Soon the sound came closer. "This horse is going too fast," a female voice yelled.

A horse rushed past them with Alicia on its back.

"Can someone help me? Please?" she shouted as she passed them.

Jeremy kicked his horse and started to chase after her.

Chapter Nine

Eden watched Jeremy ride after Alicia, trying to convince herself Alicia was actually in danger and not setting up some elaborate way to get Jeremy's attention. Again. As hard as she tried to believe otherwise, she was certain this was one more of Alicia's tricks.

Sophie and Antonio rode up next to Eden. "Poor Alicia, she must be so scared," Sophie said.

"Jeremy will help her," Antonio said. "He's a horse expert. Been riding all his life."

Maybe Eden had misjudged the situation. She didn't want Alicia to get hurt.

"He's still chasing her." Sophie pointed. "I hope he can catch her. I wonder why the horse took off like that."

The guy from the stable rushed past them, kicking his horse.

"I thought he said all the horses were tame and gentle," Eden said.

"He did. I'm not sure what got into this one." Sophie bit her lip. "I only wanted everyone to have an enjoyable ride."

"Don't worry, baby. Alicia will be fine," Antonio said.

"I hope so." Sophie sounded worried.

Eden was feeling even worse for her accusatory thoughts. Maybe

Alicia had really been in danger. Regardless, Jeremy was pretty amazing for going after her.

"Look, they've stopped," Antonio said, pointing ahead.

"Oh, I'm so relieved," Sophie said, then let out a long breath.

They rode the horses for and caught up to Alicia, who was by then surrounded by some of the other members of the wedding party.

"I was terrified when the horse bolted. Thankfully, Jeremy came to my rescue." Alicia looked at him with big doe-eyes. "Thank you for saving my life."

Eden tried to push down the unsympathetic thoughts that rose up. What did it matter anyway? She wasn't in some sort of competition with Alicia. Sure, Jeremy was handsome and easy to talk to, and she enjoyed being around him, but the weekend would be over and only a memory soon enough. Eden told herself it wasn't worth getting worked up about it.

"I'm so relieved you're okay," Sophie said. "Thanks, Jeremy for saving her."

"It really wasn't that big of a deal," he said as he shot a glance Eden's way.

"Are you kidding?" Alicia wrapped her arm around him. "I don't know what would've happened if you hadn't been here to help me."

"I thought you said she rode horses a lot," Antonio whispered to Sophie, but Eden heard him.

"She did. But this one must've spooked or something."

Or something. Eden watched Alicia fall all over Jeremy. She still had her suspicions that the horse taking off was a trick, but she reminded herself she wasn't going to get sucked into any drama.

Jeremy walked over to Eden and looked up at her. "Do you need some help getting off the horse?"

Eden shook her head. Jeremy didn't need to rescue two damsels. She could certainly get off this horse by herself. "I'm fine. But, thank you anyway." Eden swung her left leg behind her to get down and the horse took a couple steps. *What are you doing, horse? Hold still.* She tried again to swing her left leg, but the animal shifted its weight.

"Try the other side," Jeremy said.

Eden looked at him perplexed.

He walked around to the left of the horse. "Generally, you dismount the horse on this side."

Eden swung her right leg this time, but somehow got her left foot entangled in the stirrup. Before she knew it, she was in Jeremy's arms.

"Uh, what happened?" she asked, a little dazed.

"I didn't want you to fall, so I caught you."

For a moment their gazes locked. Blood rushed through Eden's veins and settled in her cheeks while her heartbeat accelerated. "I think you can put me down now."

"Oh. Yeah. Of course." Jeremy set her down gently.

"Thanks." They were standing so close to each other Eden could smell the faint scent of cinnamon on his breath. She sucked in a ragged breath.

"Anytime," he said.

She cautioned herself not to focus on his full lips. Or to think about what it would feel like to kiss them.

"Jeremy?" came the all-too-familiar screech.

"I think Alicia needs you again," Eden said, hoping it didn't sound snide.

Jeremy blinked, then took a step back.

"Oh, there you are," Alicia said in her shrill voice. "My knight in shining armor, who came to my rescue."

"I did what anyone would have," Jeremy said. His humility was endearing.

"Hey, everyone," Sophie said. "We're going to have a picnic dinner, then we'll have the wedding rehearsal."

"I love picnics. Don't you, Jeremy?" Alicia said, completely ignoring Eden.

"Follow Antonio and me to our picnic spot, everyone." Antonio pulled Sophie in for a kiss and she laughed, then playfully slapped him on the chest. "If you keep doing that we'll never get to our dinner."

Eden watched them. She exhaled and let her shoulders relax. What would it be like to be loved like that?

"Lucky, aren't they?" Jeremy said behind her, breaking into her thoughts and making her jump.

Before she could respond, Alicia called out, "All the bridesmaids need to come here pronto."

"I guess that means me," Eden said to Jeremy. She reluctantly walked over to Alicia and the other women.

"I've made arrangements with the hotel to go in and decorate the bridal suite for the wedding night. Can y'all help me?"

Everyone nodded.

"We want to make this a special night for Sophie."

"I can get some rose petals," one of the women said.

"And I'll get candles," another one said.

"Perfect," Alicia said.

"I can get some chocolates," Eden said. "Sophie loves dark chocolate."

"Hmm. I don't know about that. I think we'll skip chocolates," Alicia said.

Seriously? It was so obvious this woman didn't like Eden. And for no other reason except that Jeremy talked to her. Were they in high school still, or what? Eden didn't know how much more she could take. She glanced over at Sophie and Antonio snuggled up together. *I guess I can take all I need to for her.* She wasn't going to ruin this weekend for her best friend no matter how childish Alicia acted.

"Keep thinking about what else we can do and we'll pow-wow again tomorrow," Alicia said.

They all walked over to an area with tables decorated with lavender tablecloths and fresh flowers. Another longer table was at one end with bowls of salad and platters of fried chicken. Eden took a plate. She added potato salad, cole slaw, and two buttermilk biscuits to her chicken, which made her mouth water. She couldn't wait to eat.

"Fried chicken is one of my favorite meals," Jeremy said as he walked up next to her. "Reminds me of my grandma."

"She used to make it?"

"Yes. She'd make it for the whole family. And it was delicious," he said.

It wasn't hard to picture Jeremy sitting at a table surrounded by family after a hard day's work on the ranch.

They walked over to a table and sat down. Eden was tempted to see where Alicia was and prepare herself for another intrusion, but she resisted and hoped for the best.

"Sounds like you had the kind of childhood most people only dream about. Living on a ranch, riding horses, family meals." Eden tore off a piece of her buttermilk biscuit and stuck it in her mouth.

"I guess it was pretty idyllic." Jeremy said it as if he'd never thought of it that way before.

She studied him. "You miss it, don't you?"

He nodded. "I miss the simple life. Dallas is busy and crazy most of the time. There are people everywhere. It's a constant rush."

"Do you like Dallas?" She was curious to hear his answer.

"I like things about living there." He shrugged. "But I miss the quiet of a country night. And looking up at the sky with millions of stars. And the wide-open spaces." He gazed out toward the ocean.

"You're definitely living in the wrong place, then."

"Maybe I am." He took a bite of his chicken. After he swallowed it, he said, "Something's been off with my life in Dallas. I hadn't thought about it much until now." He looked at her. "You've helped me see things a little more clearly."

"I have?"

He nodded. "I may not be cut out for city life, after all."

She didn't mean to make him rethink his life or anything. She was simply asking a question. If her question helped him solve something, then she was glad.

They chatted more and finished their meal.

"I think we have some time to ourselves. How about if we take a walk?" Jeremy said.

"Sure." *How long will it be before Alicia intrudes? I give her less than ten minutes.*

They started toward the ocean, twilight beginning to darken the sky. The sand was still warm beneath her feet and the moist air wrapped around her.

"The beach here is different than in Oregon," she said.

"How so?" Jeremy looked at her. Even in the dimming light, it was easy to see his strong jaw and magnetic eyes.

"The water is much bluer and colder in Oregon," she said, continuing to walk closer to the water and hoping he might reach out for her hand.

"Do you make it to the coast often?"

"I've been a few times. It's pretty." She enjoyed living in Oregon and didn't plan to move for a long time.

Jeremy stooped down and grasped something from the sand. "Is this yours?" He held up Eden's silver bracelet.

"Yes. Thank you."

He smiled and put it back on her wrist.

"I can't believe it fell off. Or that you spotted it. Thank you." She was glad she didn't lose her bracelet.

They made it to the edge of the sea water. Eden watched as the cool water rushed around her feet and swallowed them.

"The beach is great," Jeremy said, plunging his hands into his pockets. "But I'm more of a mountain guy."

An image of Jeremy with a day's stubble and dressed in a flannel shirt popped into Eden's mind. Next, she and Jeremy were sitting in front of a cozy fire entwined in each other's arms. *Stop it.* Winter fantasies with this man were not acceptable. She shook her head to dislodge it.

Jeremy looked at her as if he knew what she was thinking.

She took a few more steps into the swirling water. Changing the subject, she asked, "What do you like to do with your free time? Besides write songs, of course." It was still so attractive that he wrote songs and played instruments.

"I like to fish, but I don't do much fishing in Dallas." He took his hands out of his pockets and held them up. "I like to build things like bookcases and tables."

"Do you do much of that?" What couldn't this man do?

He shrugged.

She tried to read him, but wasn't sure, so she said, "Are you a workaholic?"

He laughed. "I do work a lot."

They walked deeper into the water so it was almost to Eden's knees. The water felt soft and smooth on her legs. Suddenly, she stepped on something sharp, "Ouch."

"Are you okay?" Jeremy stopped and looked at her.

"There's something sharp in the water." She took another step, but then almost collapsed when her foot hit whatever it was again.

Jeremy reached out and steadied her, then in one swift move she was in his arms again. "Maybe you stepped on some glass."

His strong, capable arms carried her out of the water and toward the sand. Her face was so close to his it made her heart skip several beats. He placed her carefully on the beach and for a moment, time stood still.

"Let me look at your foot." His gentle hands moved from her calf down to her foot. He took out his phone and used the flashlight in inspect her foot. "I can see some blood where you cut it, but it isn't too much."

"I can't believe I've cut my foot right before Sophie's wedding."

"I don't think it'll be a problem. It'll probably stop bleeding any minute. I can go find a bandage," he offered.

"I'm sure it'll be fine." She didn't want him to leave. A warning voice sounded in her head, but she silenced it.

He sat next to her and leaned back on his elbows. "Sure is a perfect night. Antonio and Sophie couldn't have picked a better weekend to get married."

Eden gazed out toward the horizon. "I'm glad I came."

Softly, he said, "I'm glad you came too."

What felt like the flutter of a thousand wings stirred inside her stomach.

"Eden?" Sophie's voice rang out down the beach.

Eden waved her arms.

Sophie ran toward them. When she reached them, she looked at Eden, then at Jeremy. "Oh. I'm interrupting."

Eden didn't want to make Sophie feel bad, so she said, "I stepped on something in the water and Jeremy brought me up here."

"Is it serious?" Sophie drew her brows together.

Eden shook her head. "I don't think so."

Sophie bent down and looked over Eden's foot. "Probably a crab. That happens all the time on this beach."

"A crab?" Eden said, picturing an orange crustacean with huge pincers.

Sophie waved her hand. "When I was a kid we'd step on them all the time."

Jeremy placed his hand on her foot and it sent a ribbon of warmth all the way up her leg. "It looks good now," he said.

"Are you saying my leg looks good?" Eden said with a lift to her brow.

Jeremy gave her a knowing smile.

"Okay, you two, we need to get back for the rehearsal." Sophie stood and started walking back.

Jeremy stood, then offered his hand to Eden. She took it and he pulled her up, but didn't let go of her hand.

They walked back toward the group holding hands and Eden basked in the light, airy feeling she had while she was with Jeremy. It felt so easy and so natural to be together.

They followed Sophie to a narrow path and Jeremy dropped Eden's hand. "I'll walk first to make sure the path is safe," he said.

"He's such a gentleman," Sophie whispered behind her cupped hand. "Don't you think?"

Sophie was so transparent.

They walked along the path until it opened into a lighted area. Eden stayed back as she watched Alicia rush over to Jeremy.

"Where have you been?" Alicia asked as if her life depended on his answer. "I've been looking all over for you."

"On the beach," Jeremy said.

"Why didn't you tell me? I would've gone with you."

"I wasn't alone."

Eden bit her lip so she wouldn't smile. As she and Sophie emerged from the path, Alicia straightened, then marched away.

Eden stood next to Jeremy. "I think you made her mad."

"I didn't mean to," he said, shrugging a shoulder.

"Okay, everyone let's head over for the rehearsal." Sophie motioned for them to move toward the parking lot.

Chapter Ten

Eden rode with Sophie and Antonio over to the rehearsal dinner, but Jeremy ended up in a different car. *No doubt Alicia maneuvered him into the same car as her.* Eden tamped down the jealousy that tried to surface when she thought about Jeremy being in the same car as Alicia. She chastised herself for letting Alicia suck her into this silly game.

"So, tell me," Sophie said, twisting to look at Eden in the backseat.

"Tell you what?" Eden played dumb.

"You and Jeremy seem to be getting along very well." A grin enveloped Sophie's face.

"I guess you could say that." It was true. They were getting to know each other and spending time together. Except Alicia kept getting in the way. Part of her wanted to let Alicia have it, but the other part wondered if Jeremy liked Alicia's attention.

"You like him?" Sophie arched a brow.

"I don't dislike him." Eden wasn't about to fall into something with Jeremy. Something she couldn't even define. A friendly, flirty weekend that would never go anywhere? A friendship? The beginning of something more?

"But you'd go out with him? After this weekend?" Sophie's eyes were wide and expectant.

"Yes, Soph, I'd go out with him." Eden shrugged. "Are you happy now?"

"He's a solid guy," Antonio said. "He's got a good head on his shoulders and he's a genuinely nice person."

Sophie raised her hands up and pumped them in the air a few times. "I'd love it if the two of you got together."

"You are such a hopeless romantic," Eden said, playing with her bracelet and letting her thoughts go back to the beach with Jeremy.

"They make a gorgeous couple, too. Don't you think, mi amor?" Sophie turned to her fiancé.

Antonio nodded.

Eden had to laugh at Sophie's enthusiasm.

"I knew you'd be a good match," Sophie sang out.

When they got back to the hotel, Eden couldn't stop herself from searching for Jeremy, but he was nowhere in sight. They walked through the hotel lobby out to the beach where the ceremony was set to take place the next evening. Sophie and Antonio met a man who Eden assumed was the one who'd perform the ceremony. When she heard voices, she turned to a group of people, including Jeremy and Alicia. With Alicia hanging on his arm, Eden had to more than wonder if Jeremy wanted to pursue Alicia.

Even if he and Eden had had some great conversations, and even if there was an undeniable spark between them, if he wanted to be with Alicia he should. Because that meant he wasn't someone Eden would want to date anyway.

The group made its way over.

Feeling miffed, Eden deliberately didn't make eye contact with Jeremy. She wasn't interested in getting her feelings yanked around this weekend. Or any weekend.

"This is Pastor Thompson. He's going to perform the ceremony," Sophie said. "We need everyone to line up back there." Sophie pointed behind the wedding party. She spread her arms out in front of her and said, "We'll have chairs set up here. And an arch right here. We'll also have some tiki torches around. We have a string quartet that will be playing music over there." She pointed to a spot. "When the bridal march begins, you two will start down the aisle together." She pointed to one of the groomsmen and one of the bridesmaids. She continued to match up men and women.

"Eden and Jeremy will walk down together, then take their places. Let's practice that." Sophie said.

They all lined up as Sophie had instructed. The pastor stood with his back to the ocean.

"Okay. Imagine the chairs are all set up and the march has begun." Sophie started humming the music and using her arms to conduct the wedding party. When it came time for Eden and Jeremy to walk together, an obvious set-up from Sophie, Eden threaded her arm through his and they walked down the aisle, then separated when they got to where Sophie stood. Sophie rushed to the back and practiced her march to Antonio at the front.

While they practiced their vows, Eden snuck a glance at Jeremy, who was looking right at her. He said he wasn't interested in Alicia, but his actions seemed to indicate otherwise, which left Eden so confused. She blew out a breath. The last thing she wanted was to become all involved in some weekend love triangle. After the wedding she'd go home and never see Jeremy or Alicia again. It so wasn't worth it. At least that's what she kept telling herself.

Her phone vibrated and she pulled it out to see who was calling. It was her assistant, Jessica. She decided to answer it, so she stepped away from the rehearsal.

"Hello?"

"Eden, we have a problem."

"What?" Eden's heart started to beat faster.

"I know you're at a friend's wedding, but the Sidwell children have been pulled from their foster home." Jessica sounded upset.

"Why?" Eden thought everything with this placement was going well.

"Adam Evans was arrested for a DUI."

"Are you serious?" Eden wanted to scream. How could this man be so irresponsible as to be driving under the influence? He'd made a commitment to these kids. Now, one more person had let them down.

"Unbelievable, right?" Eden could hear the irritation in Jessica's voice.

"So, what should we do?" There wasn't much Eden could do from Texas, but the Sidwells needed help.

"We need an emergency home," Jessica said.

"Should I come back?" She didn't want to leave Sophie, but her heart was heavy. Ellie and Josiah would be so frightened. She wanted to rush home and comfort them and find them a safe place to live, because they'd already seen too much in their young lives. Why did people have to make such awful choices that hurt children?

"You have your wedding. I can take care of this, but I needed your approval."

Feeling torn, Eden said, "You have approval to place them in one of our emergency foster homes. But maybe I should fly back tomorrow."

"No. I think it'll be fine. You'll be back in a few days."

"I feel so bad for the kids. They've had such a rough time. I thought this was going to work out for them. I'm so mad at Adam for ruining it." Feeling disappointed and outraged, she said, "What was he thinking?"

"He wasn't. It's a mess, but we have to take care of the kids," Jessica said.

"I agree. The kids come first, so get them to a safe place. The Camdens are available, I believe, and they're always willing to take emergency cases." Eden was grateful for a handful of families that would fill in during times like this.

"I'll call them. I'm sorry to bother you, Eden."

"Don't worry about it. I appreciate you finding them a new home. Thank you," Eden said, thankful for Jessica and her willingness to step in while Eden was gone.

Eden ended the call, her stomach tied up in knots. *Those poor kids. I wish I could adopt them myself.*

"Is everything okay?" Jeremy asked, jolting her from her thoughts.

"Oh, it's work." She smoothed her hair. "Some kids need an emergency placement."

He raised his eyebrows. "That doesn't sound good. Why?"

"The foster dad was arrested for a DUI."

Jeremy shook his head. "That's so unfair to the kids."

"It is. It's so frustrating and heartbreaking to see so many kids suffering because of the choices of the adults in their lives. I mean, these are children. They need love and stability. Why do the adults have to be like this? Why is it so hard to take care of kids?" Angry tears stung her eyes.

Jeremy reached out and pulled her into a hug. Without thinking about it, she melted into his embrace.

"I'm sorry. I didn't mean to . . ."

"Care about children?" he said.

She stepped back and wiped at her eyes. "Maybe I'm too involved."

"How can you be too involved when it comes to kids? All kids deserve to feel loved and deserve to feel safe. It's good they have people like you to care about them," Jeremy said with fervor. "What you do matters."

It felt good to be validated. "Sometimes, I get a little too passionate about my work."

He gazed at her, making her breath catch in her throat. "You can't be too passionate when it comes to helping kids."

She studied him. "Sounds like you might have some experience yourself."

He shrugged. "My aunt and uncle died in a car accident and left my two nephews. My parents didn't want them in the system, so they adopted them when I was a kid."

"Wow." She jerked her head back. "That must've been hard for everyone."

"It was, I guess, but having two extra brothers was a lot of fun." His smile reached up to his eyes.

"Not all kids are that lucky." Eden knew this better than most people.

He brushed a stray hair from her face. "The kids that have you in their corner are very lucky."

His gaze captured hers and the tips of her ears warmed. An urge to kiss him enveloped her and all she could think about was kissing him.

"Eden and Jeremy, let's go through it one more time," Sophie said, breaking into the moment.

Eden cleared her throat, then stepped back. She took her place with everyone else. This time as she and Jeremy walked up the aisle, something passed between them. She felt a connection to him in way she hadn't with anyone else before. It was exciting, but also a little unnerving.

After they finished, Sophie announced everyone had free time for the rest of the night. "Don't forget, girls, we have massages in the morning, then our nail appointments. We need to get ready before the ceremony at six o'clock."

Eden wasn't much for pampering herself. She preferred to save her money, but since Sophie had already paid for everything she planned to enjoy it and make lots of memories with Sophie tomorrow.

Jeremy made his way over to her. "Are you interested in a late-night dessert by the pool?"

"Maybe." She gave him a slight smile.

He stepped closer to her. "What can I do to convince you?"

"Does it involve chocolate?" Eden was a certified choc-a-holic.

He leaned in and whispered in her ear. "That depends. Do you like chocolate?"

She nodded.

"Then, yes, it involves a lot of chocolate." His warm breath tickled her ear and sent a shiver down her spine.

She stepped back and looked at him. "In that case, my answer is yes."

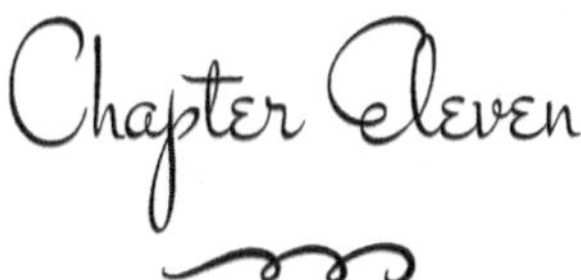

Chapter Eleven

Eden and Jeremy walked over to the pool area and sat in chairs in the restaurant area, then ordered a piece of black forest cake with extra chocolate sauce to share. "You seem to be distracted," he said.

"I'm sorry." She waved her hand. "I'm worried about those kids. I wish I could adopt all the kids I work with."

Jeremy smiled.

"What?" She twirled a piece of her hair.

"You have a huge heart. I don't meet many women who'd want to adopt a bunch of kids."

"I've always loved kids. I used to ask women in the neighborhood if I could babysit their kids for free." She laughed.

He leaned back. "Where do you see yourself in five years?"

"Hmm, that's an interesting question." She crossed her legs. "I'd like to be married and begin a family. How about you?"

"The same." He cast a glance over at the almost-newlyweds. "Watching Sophie and Antonio has definitely given me hope."

"They've been in love for so long. I'm happy they're finally getting married."

The waitress brought them their cake.

"Wow, that looks scrumptious." Eden hadn't seen so much chocolatey goodness on one plate in a long time.

Jeremy handed her a fork. "Dive in."

Eden plunged her fork into the cake, then put it her mouth where it melted into chocolate heaven. "It tastes even better than it looks," she said. "I could live on this."

Jeremy smiled. "So, you live in Portland, you love children and chocolate, and you're afraid of horses. Anything else?" He took a bite of the cake.

She tapped the fork on the plate. "I have a black belt in karate."

Jeremy's eyes widened. "Really? I didn't see that coming."

She grinned inwardly at his reaction. "I'm a woman of mystery." She laughed.

"I'd say you are a woman of great interest."

She swallowed hard, then gazed at him across the half-eaten piece of cake. "I am?"

"Definitely." He said it with such certainty.

She hadn't expected to meet someone at Sophie's wedding, especially not someone like Jeremy. But, she reminded herself, it couldn't really go anywhere.

"There you are," Sophie said as she and Antonio approached them.

"What are you two doing?" Eden said.

"We're saying goodnight." She flung her arms around Antonio's neck. "Tomorrow I will be Mrs. Antonio Vega." She kissed him. "Tonight is my last night as a single lady."

Eden wanted to spend more time with Jeremy, but she felt like she should go with Sophie. "I'll go up to the room with you."

"Oh, no. You stay here. I don't want to interrupt . . . anything." Sophie raised her eyebrows up and down.

Eden shook her head and hoped Jeremy was oblivious to Sophie's insinuation. "We're done." She glanced at Jeremy, who wore a disappointed, but understanding expression. At least she hoped he understood. This was her best friend who was getting married tomorrow and she needed to spend this time with her.

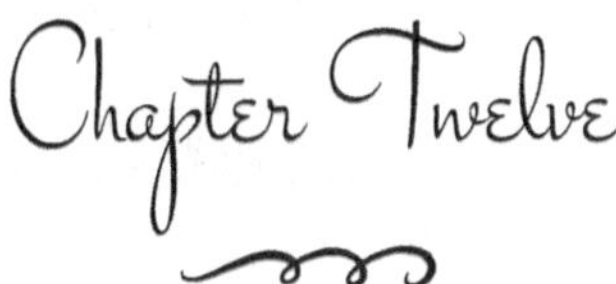

Chapter Twelve

Jeremy watched Eden walk away with Sophie. He wanted to ask her to stay, but he didn't want to interfere with their "girl thing."

"She's a good one," Antonio said.

"You're a lucky man, my friend." Jeremy nodded.

"Oh, yeah. I am the luckiest man. But I wasn't talking about Sophie." He pointed at Jeremy.

"Huh?"

"Eden. She's a fantastic woman. Been a good friend for years."

A waitress with a long, black braid came over to the table. "Can I get you anything, gentlemen?" She smiled.

"No, thanks. This cake was enough for me," Jeremy said, pushing the plate away and still wishing Eden was there with him.

"Let me know if you change your mind." The waitress gathered up the plate.

"Why haven't you told me about Eden before?" Jeremy asked Antonio.

Antonio shrugged. "Guess I didn't think too much about it since she lives in Oregon."

"That is a long way away." Jeremy sat back, his mind mulling over options.

"You like her." Antonio grinned. "Sophie thought you would."

"Yeah, I do." He massaged his neck. "She isn't like the other women I've met in Dallas."

"Then do something about it, man." Antonio tapped the table with his hand. "Don't let her slip through your fingers."

"Any suggestions?" Jeremy was open to ideas. It wasn't like he could date her regularly. When would he even see her again?

"Here you are," Alicia said. "If I didn't know better, I'd think you might be hiding from me." She chuckled, then sat in a chair next to Jeremy.

Antonio checked his watch. "Some of the guys are meeting in half an hour. You know, a bachelor party of sorts." Antonio laughed. "But not too late." He stood. "See you in the lobby?"

Jeremy glanced up at him, "I'll be there."

Antonio left.

"I'm glad he got the hint," Alicia said. "Now it's only me and you." She snuggled up to him.

"About that." How could he tell Alicia he wasn't at all interested without being rude or hurting her feelings?

"Now don't say anything. Let's just have some fun." She rubbed his shoulder.

"That's the thing."

Alicia ran her fingers through Jeremy's hair, then said, "We shouldn't waste this time together." She left her hand on his arm.

Jeremy had had enough. He removed her hand from his arm. "Alicia, you are a beautiful girl."

"I'm not a girl. I'm a woman. And I can prove it." She licked her lips.

"I don't want you to prove it." He pushed out a breath. "I'm really not interested."

"What?" Alicia sounded indignant.

"You seem to be a nice girl—woman—but I don't have any interest in—"

"Because you're into that Eden?" She said it with such derision.

"This doesn't have anything to do with anyone else. You and I aren't a good match." He was trying to be as diplomatic as possible.

Alicia narrowed her eyes. "I'm not used to being turned down."

"I'm sorry." What else could he say?

Alicia reached over and grabbed a glass of water, then drenched him with the water. "That's what I think of you." She turned and stomped off.

Jeremy wiped at his wet face. Being soaked with ice water was worth it if it meant Alicia was finally going to leave him alone. Now he could focus the time they had left this weekend on Eden.

<h1 style="text-align: center;">Chapter Thirteen</h1>

Once they were inside the elevator, Sophie said, "Things are sure heating up between the two of you." She slung her arm around Eden. "I'd rather you spend time with Jeremy than with me. I should probably get some sleep anyway. Except I'm way too excited for tomorrow." She bounced up and down a few times.

"Sophie, I've missed you," Eden said. "If I had one word to describe you, it'd be enthusiastic." Eden couldn't help but feed off Sophie's positive energy.

"And if I had one word to describe you, it'd be compassionate. You have the biggest heart of anyone I know."

"Aww, thanks." Eden hugged her. "That's sweet."

"I think someone else has noticed too." Rubbing her hands together, Sophie said, "So you and Jeremy will see each other after this weekend, right?"

Eden shrugged. "I don't know about that." Jeremy seemed to be amazing, but that voice in her head reminded her of all the broken relationships she'd seen. It was risky to get involved, especially with a man whom she'd just met.

"Why not?"

"Lots of reasons. Like he lives in Texas and I live in Oregon for one."

That seemed to be a pretty big deterrent to anything happening after this weekend anyway, even if he was a truly decent guy.

"Who cares?" Sophie waved her hand. "What does a little distance matter when it comes to affairs of the heart."

Eden shook her head and smiled at Sophie's romantic notions. "There isn't an Antonio for everyone, you know."

"Are you going to blame me for wanting all of my friends to feel the way I do, especially my best friend?"

"Nope. I can't blame you for that." Love seemed so simple through Sophie's eyes.

"Maybe you and Jeremy can have the same thing?" Sophie said.

"I think you're getting way too ahead of yourself. We barely met."

Sophie placed her hand on her hip. "And I suppose you're going to tell me you aren't falling for him?"

"Falling for him?" Eden liked him. But Sophie already had them in love and married with a couple of kids. Eden wasn't even close to thinking about that.

Sophie grinned. "Maybe I should be a professional matchmaker."

Before they got to the room, Eden glanced at her wrist. "Oh, no, my bracelet is missing." She looked around the floor.

"I wonder where it could be?" Sophie said as she glanced around.

"I remember I had it when we came over here for the rehearsal."

"Maybe it fell off downstairs?"

"Could've been during the rehearsal or by the pool." The bracelet could be anywhere.

"You should go look for it," Sophie said. "Maybe someone found it and turned it in."

Eden nodded. "I'll be right back."

She rushed down to the lobby. When she gazed over at the restaurant area, she saw Alicia and Jeremy talking. From where Eden was, they looked pretty cozy. Too cozy, actually. Was Jeremy encouraging both of them? Playing them? A surge of anger bubbled up and Eden's face heated. How dare he be so brazen. She was done with this little game once and for all.

Eden hurried back upstairs, her heart beating fast. She knew better. It seemed that if he were interested in anything with her, it must be a fling. And Eden wasn't a fling girl. He was better off with Alicia if that were the case.

"Did you find your bracelet?" Sophie asked as Eden walked into the room.

Eden shook her head, still irritated at seeing Jeremy and Alicia together.

"What's wrong?" Sophie studied Eden.

"Nothing." Eden pasted on a smile. She didn't want to argue with Sophie about Jeremy or Alicia or whatever was obviously going on between them. It wasn't the time or place.

"Are you sure?"

"Absolutely. I'm super excited for you. You've found your Prince Charming. And you're marrying him tomorrow." Eden wanted Sophie to focus on her special day.

"I am!" Sophie fell dramatically on the bed. "Which is why I don't want to have some crazy night tonight. I want to be well-rested for my wonderful day tomorrow and look beautiful for him."

"He'd think you were beautiful, no matter what," Eden said. Good men were hard to find, especially at your best friend's wedding.

Sophie let out a long breath. "I really want you to come visit us in Dallas. See our condo. Hangout."

"I will."

Sophie leaned up on an elbow. "Promise?"

A knock sounded. "Who is that?" Sophie asked. She went to the door and opened it. The other bridesmaids stumbled inside.

"Hey, cuz, why aren't we out celebrating your wedding tomorrow?" Alicia burped.

"You're drunk." Sophie shook her head.

"Yeah." Alicia nodded.

"We've been down with the guys," Gabrielle said. "That Jeremy is a hottie, for sure." She whistled. "Right, Alicia?"

They started laughing.

Eden tried to ignore the flare of agitation and resentment. If Jeremy wanted to party it up with these women, he was welcome to. Eden didn't have any hold over him. She must've misread the situation between her and Jeremy, and the connection she felt must've been fleeting. Or one-sided. Or something.

The girls continued to talk about Jeremy and one of the other groomsmen, Esteban. Eden wanted to kick them out of the room and tell them to all get lost, especially Alicia with her donkey-sounding laugh that made Eden's nerves explode. Instead, she sat and listened to their incessant chatter because Sophie obviously wanted to talk to them.

Finally, Sophie said, "Okay, girls, I need my beauty sleep. I have to look gorgeous tomorrow. Y'all need to go to your rooms." She stood and motioned for them to leave.

"Oh, come on, let's stay up. The night is young," Gabrielle said. She started doing some dance moves.

"Yeah, let's stay up," Alicia said, bumping into Sophie.

"Nope. Out of my room." Sophie opened her door and pushed them out. After she shut the door, she said, "Wow, my cousins are crazy."

Eden had another word, but she didn't voice it.

"I'm going to wash my face and brush my teeth," Sophie said. She went into the bathroom.

Eden lay on her bed staring at the ceiling. An errant tear trickled down her cheek. She'd been a fool to think Jeremy felt anything for her. A total fool. He was a player, like most of the men she'd interacted with personally and professionally. For a hot second, she thought maybe he was different. She closed her eyes, looking forward to the wedding and then the time she could go home to her normal, predictable life where her heart was safe.

Chapter Fourteen

"Oh, no," Sophie screamed, waking Eden from a deep sleep. Sophie threw her covers off and jumped out of bed.

Eden sat up still a little dazed. "What? Is something wrong?"

"We overslept. We have our facials, and massages, and nails. We have to get going." Sophie rushed frantically around the room.

Eden yawned and rubbed the sleep from her eyes. She hoped to avoid Jeremy as much as possible today. That would probably be easy since he'd most likely spend his time with Alicia—at least that's how it sounded last night.

"We'll have to skip breakfast," Sophie said, grabbing a blue print dress from the closet.

Eden's stomach growled in protest. "Are we sure?"

"No time." Sophie looked at her. "We need to get ready right now."

"How did we oversleep?" Eden yawned again and stretched her arms.

"I thought I set my alarm." Sophie pulled out her phone and tapped in a number. "Hey, Gabs, are you up? We need to get going. Meet us in the lobby in fifteen minutes."

Eden rose from her bed and dressed in a cream lace skirt and coral blouse. Her stomach was yelling at her to eat. She barely had enough time to brush her hair and teeth and swipe on a little mascara before Sophie was standing in the doorway of the bathroom staring at her.

"Let's go," Sophie said.

When they rode the elevator to the lobby, Eden tensed at the thought of seeing Jeremy. As the doors opened, there he stood next to Antonio.

"There you are, my beautiful bride," Antonio said.

"You can't see me today." Sophie held her hands up in front of her. "If my mother finds, she'll flip. You know how she is about traditions."

"I saw her earlier. She went to get her hair done with your grandma." Antonio swept her up in his arms.

"No, no, no." Sophie protested. She wiggled out of his embrace. "This is bad luck. Pretend you didn't see me."

Eden avoided eye contact with Jeremy.

Sophie grabbed Eden's hand. "We're going to be pampered. I'll see you later today."

"But—"

"Antonio, I mean it." Sophie's voice was firm.

Sophie rushed out of the hotel dragging Eden behind her.

"I can't believe he saw me before the wedding," Sophie said as they got into a taxi. "My mother cannot find out. She'll make a huge deal out of it."

"I'll be fine. Really. You have nothing to worry about," Eden said, hoping to reassure her.

"We're supposed to be getting our massages in ten minutes. I hope the others are already there." Sophie tapped her fingers on her leg.

"Where to?" the driver asked.

"Seaside Massage and Spa, please." Sophie sat back and exhaled with a whoosh.

"You need to relax," Eden said. Sophie was way too stressed.

"I know, I know. I didn't think I'd be so nervous today. This is my wedding day." Sophie let out a squeal. "I can't believe it's finally here."

"And it will be a perfect day. The weather will be wonderful and you will be the most beautiful bride ever." Eden reached over and placed her hand on Sophie's. "Relax."

Sophie squeezed Eden's hand. "Thanks. You know, you're the sister I never had."

Sophie's words made Eden tear up. "Back at you." She smiled.

They arrived at the spa.

Inside the building, the walls were painted a light blue with some foam green accents. Instrumental music played in the background and a soft floral scent floated through the air.

Sophie looked around. "Where are the others?"

Eden walked over to the desk. "We're with a bridal party." She pointed at Sophie. "This is the bride."

"Oh, yes. We took some of the women to the back for their facials. We can do your massages now," said a petite woman with shoulder-length black hair.

"Perfect," Sophie said.

Eden lay on a table. A woman came in and began kneading her muscles. Eden started to relax. Having a massage was heavenly. She wished she could afford to have one every day. Her breathing slowed and soon she was so relaxed her limbs felt like overcooked noodles. Thoughts from yesterday swirled around her mind. An image of Jeremy's handsome face popped in. Feelings of warmth welled up inside her, but she pushed them back down, because there was no point. He'd seemed interested in her, but then he'd spent time with Alicia. And, from the looks of it, he preferred Sophie's young cousin.

After several more minutes of the massage, the woman aid, "If you'll follow me, we'll get you ready for your facial. You can put on the robe in the room."

Eden waited in a small room after dressing in the supplied white, terry cloth robe. She could overhear the conversation in the next room. "I'm so excited. Jeremy said he's going to come visit me in San Antonio." There was no mistaking Alicia's nails-on-a-chalkboard voice.

"He's so hot." Eden wasn't sure who was talking, but she suspected it was Gabrielle.

"I know. Isn't he? And he's the best kisser. Oh, those lips."

Eden's heartbeat thudded in her ears. Jeremy had kissed Alicia? Seriously? She didn't want to hear anymore, but couldn't leave, so she sat and listened, anger building inside. She wasn't so mad at Jeremy as she was at herself. She knew better, but she'd ignored her warning voice. She'd obviously misread him and thought there was some kind of a connection between them. *Wrong, wrong, wrong.* Letting out a long, but silent, breath, she vowed to get through this day, then forget she'd ever met him.

The woman with black hair came back to the room. "You can follow me now."

In the room, Sophie lounged on a chair with her head back. "Eden, this is so awesome. We're going to be gorgeous."

Eden didn't say anything. Her feelings were all jumbled up inside. She sat on the chair and tried to shut out any and all thoughts of Jeremy as the woman smeared the cream on her face.

After they finished the facials, Eden put her clothes back on and walked out to the lobby.

"Oh, hi, Eden," Alicia said with a smirk. "How did you like your massage and your facial?"

As if Alicia cares. "Where's Soph?" Eden asked, not interested in any immature banter with Alicia.

"She's coming out any minute," Gabrielle said. "Then it's time to get our nails done."

Eden gave them a plastic smile. *For Sophie I can endure this.*

Sophie walked out with a grin as wide as the Gulf of Mexico. "I have directions to the nail salon. Isn't this so fun?" she said.

Eden nodded, but she'd rather walk ten miles with glass shards in her shoes than spend more time with Alicia.

At the nail salon, Alicia said, "I want my nails to be perfect today." She smirked and flipped her hair back over her shoulders.

Eden wanted to strangle her, but thought better of it. Besides, she didn't want to spend Sophie's wedding day in jail. Right? *If only.*

Forcing thoughts of Alicia from her mind, Eden focused on getting her nails done. She hadn't ever pampered herself so much, but she could get used to it. Sophie picked out the color for all the women and they got the works—a manicure and a pedicure.

Sophie checked her phone. "Okay, we're doing well on time. When we finish here, we'll go back to the hotel. I've hired a make-up artist for us."

"I can do my own," Eden offered. She wasn't much for a lot of make-up.

Sophie shook her head. "This is my wedding day and I want everyone to be gorgeous like me, including their make-up." She laughed.

After their mani-pedis the women made their way back to the hotel. When they got to the front doors, Sophie stopped. "Make sure Antonio isn't in the lobby. I for sure don't want to see him right now."

"I'll look," Alicia said.

Because, of course, she would. Eden was sure Alicia was actually looking for Jeremy. And why wouldn't she if they'd been kissing last night?

"All clear," Alicia said, then motioned for them to go inside.

Eden hurried up to the room with Sophie.

"I ordered some room service for us so we can eat while we're getting ready." Sophie sat on the bed.

Eden pulled out the flowing lavender strapless gown.

Sophie held her hand out. "Remember, we're all going barefoot on the beach."

Eden held the gown up to her. "This is so pretty. And I knew it'd be lavender."

"My favorite color. I think the dress will look stunning on you," Sophie said.

"Thanks. I can't wait to see you in your wedding dress." Eden tried to envision what it would look like on her best friend.

Someone knocked on the door. Eden hoped it wasn't Jeremy. She didn't want to see him because she had nothing to say to him.

"Can you get that?" Sophie asked.

"Sure." Eden opened the door to Sophie's mom and grandmother.

"Hello, Eden. It's so nice to see you," Sophie's mom said.

"Mrs. Winters." Eden smiled at the petite Hispanic woman. It was easy to see the resemblance between Sophie and her mother.

"Carmen, remember?" She wrapped her arms around Eden. "It's been years."

"It has," Eden said. Sophie's mom had always been kind to her. And she made the best tamales.

"This is my mother, Maria," she said with a slight accent.

"I think I met you once many years ago," Eden said to the small woman with gray hair and large brown eyes like Sophie.

"You're still a beauty," Maria said, wrinkles forming around her mouth as she smiled.

"Oh, thank you." Eden gave Sophie's grandmother a hug.

"And how about my daughter? Finally, she's getting married," Carmen said with a dramatic flair.

"Mama." Sophie rolled her eyes.

"And what a beautiful bride she will make. I hope you haven't let that groom of yours see you today." Carmen wagged her finger at Sophie.

"Of course not, Mama. That would be bad luck," Sophie said, then glanced at Eden who bit back a smile.

"Yes, it would. And we do not need that today." Carmen made a grand gesture of looking heavenward.

"Where is mi padre?" Sophie asked.

"Oh, he's around here somewhere. Probably found the bar already." Sophie's mom waved her hand, then laughed.

"He'll be ready to walk me down the aisle?" Sophie said.

"Yes, yes." Carmen walked over to Sophie and started playing with her hair. "You are wearing it up?"

"No." Sophie squared her shoulders, then said, "And we're all going barefoot."

Her mother shook her head. "Mi hija, it's bad enough you are not marrying in the church, why does it have to be so casual? Why throw away all tradition?" Carmen said with passion.

Sophie stood. "Mama, this is my wedding and this is how I want it."

"I don't understand kids these days. When I married, I did it the way my mother wanted." Carmen patted her mother's arm. "A wedding is a family affair. Why must you be so defiant?"

The tension was like molasses on a cold winter day. Eden wanted to make her escape, but Sophie gave her a pleading look. "I think it's almost time to be downstairs," Eden offered.

"Oh, yes. Mama and Abuela, can you meet us down there?"

"Are you trying to get rid of us?" Carmen said.

"No, no. I only need a few more minutes and then I'll be down."

Eden wanted to say or do something to help Sophie, but she didn't know what. Obviously, she and her mother weren't seeing eye-to-eye on this wedding.

Carmen and Maria left. As soon as Eden shut the door, Sophie let out a loud sigh. "She's so controlling."

"I'm sorry." Eden reached out and grabbed Sophie's hand.

"This is *my* wedding. I've saved for this weekend for years so it would be exactly the way that Antonio and I wanted it. My mother wants to butt in and take over. It's so frustrating." Sophie wiped at her eyes.

Eden massaged Sophie's shoulders. "You can't let it get to you. This is your special day and you look amazing. When Antonio sees you walking down the aisle he's going to realize he's the luckiest man."

Sophie hugged Eden. "I'm so glad you're here to temper all the crazy in my family."

"This wedding will be epic." Eden smiled. "And it will be exactly the way you want it."

"Thank you." Sophie sat down near the large mirror.

Eden helped Sophie put the finishing touches on her hair. "You look perfect."

"I hope so."

"Let's put on your dress." Eden helped Sophie with the gown, then stood back and admired her best friend. She was a vision of perfection in her strapless, cream-colored, empire-waisted dress.

"Does it look good?" Sophie twirled around.

"Better than good. You look magnificent." Eden had never seen a more radiant bride.

Sophie patted her cheeks. "I can't believe this is my wedding day. I've dreamed about it for so long."

Happiness filled Eden. She was thrilled she could share this day with Sophie and witness her wedding to her true love. It made Eden almost believe in fairytales.

Chapter Fifteen

Jeremy combed his hair and adjusted his lavender dress shirt. He gazed down at his khaki pants and bare feet. He wasn't sure he'd be comfortable without any shoes for the wedding, but Sophie had insisted a beach wedding meant no shoes.

He gazed at himself in the mirror. He'd been busy with Antonio all day and hadn't even seen Eden. He combed a fly away hair. He was excited for his good friend to marry the woman of his dreams, but he was also excited to see Eden again.

He hadn't expected to meet a woman like Eden this weekend. There were plenty of Alicias out in the dating scene—pretty women who were flirty and fun, but not much depth. He'd dated far too many like that and he was ready for a woman that thought about more than her hair and clothes. Someone like Eden. There was definitely a connection between them and he wanted to explore it.

He brushed his teeth and smoothed his shirt, then left his room.

Eden and Sophie took the elevator down to the lobby. Eden's heart beat faster with each floor they descended. She wasn't sure how she'd react when she saw Jeremy.

"My nerves are on fire," Sophie said. "Make sure Antonio is nowhere to be found or my mother will have a breakdown. And it won't be pretty."

Eden laughed. She'd seen Sophie's mom fired up a few times. "I'll make sure." Eden hesitated to look too much because she didn't want to face Jeremy. Sophie had made previous arrangements to keep Antonio far away from her before the ceremony, and Eden hoped both he and Jeremy would be holed up somewhere out of sight.

When Eden was sure the coast was clear, she and Sophie rushed to the room where they planned to wait with the bridesmaids until the ceremony. Once inside the room, Eden let out the breath she'd been holding. Relief washed over her. She knew she couldn't avoid Jeremy all night, but she'd take what she could get. The less she had to interact with him, the better.

Knocking thoughts of Alicia and Jeremy out of her head, Eden turned to Sophie and asked, "Can I get you anything?"

"No. I'm so nervous." Sophie shook her hands.

"Everything will be amazing," Eden said, grabbing Sophie's hands and trying to calm her.

The door opened and Alicia walked in. "You are so hot in that dress," she said. "Antonio will want to get the ceremony over as fast as possible so he can—"

"Let's keep it classy," Eden said. She'd had enough of Alicia.

"Oh, what are you, the morality police?" Alicia said, her tone full of contempt.

"Alicia, stop it," Sophie said.

Alicia rolled her eyes and left the room. Something seemed to be bothering her, but Eden wasn't about to ask her.

The other bridesmaids talked to Sophie and admired her gown.

As the minutes ticked away, Eden's stomach clenched. She was nervous for Sophie, but she was also nervous about seeing Jeremy. They'd be walking down the aisle together shortly. She hoped he wouldn't say anything to her. She wanted to erase the past two days and pretend she'd never had any interest in him. It'd be easier that way, not only because she'd be flying back to Portland tomorrow, but also because he'd chosen someone like Alicia over her. That stung.

"Are we ready in here?" a woman with red hair asked.

"Yes. I'm ready." Sophie brought her bouquet to her chest. "I'm going to marry my best friend tonight."

It was hard to feel anything but happiness around Sophie. She'd found her true love and she radiated so much exuberance, she positively glowed.

"I'll cue the musicians to begin," the woman said.

"Remember, like we rehearsed," Sophie said to her bridesmaids as they left the room.

"See you on the other side," Eden said. "You are the most beautiful bride. Ever."

Eden walked through the lobby, past the pool, then took her place as she waited to walk down the aisle. The evening was perfect. The sun was descending in the winter sky and the sea air floated on the gentle breeze while soft music played.

"Hey," Jeremy said when he walked up to Eden.

He looked handsome in his khaki pants and dress shirt with rolled up sleeves. Casual, but chic. She told her heart to stop beating so erratically, but it wouldn't listen. *Remember he was kissing Alicia last night.* "Hi," she said coolly.

"I haven't seen you all day." He smiled, and she told her stomach to ignore it.

"I've been with Sophie. And, you know, trying to keep her from seeing the groom so there isn't any bad luck." *Plus, you should be talking to Alicia, not me.*

"This is a great night for their wedding." He gazed around.

Eden nodded.

"Maybe later we can—"

"I think it's almost our turn." She wasn't about to let him suggest they see each other later. She wanted no part of whatever game he was playing.

He stuck his arm out and she looped hers around it. Touching him made it hard to breathe, but she reminded herself that she wasn't interested. At all.

They walked along the silky sand, arm-in-arm, toward the arch where Antonio stood in cream-colored pants and a cream-colored shirt with a lavender tie waiting for his bride. When they got close enough, they separated and the bridal march began. The crowd stood and turned. Sophie was dazzling as she walked down the aisle on the arm of her father.

Eden smiled, then turned and snuck a glance at Jeremy, who was staring at her. She blinked and focused her gaze back on Sophie, who joined hands with Antonio.

During the ceremony, Eden could feel Jeremy's gaze on her, but she refused to return it. Afterwards, the pastor said, "I'd like to introduce everyone to Mr. and Mrs. Vega."

Applause erupted. Antonio pulled Sophie into a long, passionate kiss, then they walked back down the aisle. *What a perfect wedding.*

Eden looked back and there was Alicia talking to Jeremy, so she rushed toward the hotel, following everyone to the room for the reception. Inside, the room was decorated with tiny white lights and round tables with white linen tablecloths. A vase with fresh cut flowers in pink, deep red, and baby's breath with a sparkly lavender ribbon adorned each table.

Another table was overflowing with food. Eden's stomach growled, so she made her way over there and piled up some prime rib, roasted potatoes, and green beans.

"I wish my daughter would have married in a church," Carmen said. "But I suppose it was nice enough."

"Sophie looked gorgeous and so ecstatic. The ceremony was simple but sweet," Eden said, defending her best friend's choice.

"Not the same as in the church by a priest, though."

Eden smiled. What else could she say? Obviously, Sophie and her mother had some unresolved issues.

Gabrielle approached them. "Aunt Carmen, it's so good to see you."

"You are looking well. Maybe a little thin," Carmen said. She hugged Gabrielle.

"Thank you. You liked the wedding?"

Carmen shrugged and Eden took this cue to find a table and sit down. She didn't look around for Jeremy, assuming he was with Alicia. In less than twenty-four hours, she'd be in Oregon and back to her regular routine, leaving all of this behind her.

A portly man with a black goatee stood at the front of the large room and said into a microphone, "We'll have dinner and dancing. Feel free to eat and dance all evening."

Behind a table and some equipment stood a short guy with a receding hairline. Eden assumed he was the DJ. He started playing some music.

"Would you care to dance?" came a deep voice from behind her.

Eden turned to see Jeremy. "Uh."

"If I didn't know better, I'd think you were avoiding me." He inclined his head toward her.

With warmed cheeks, she said, "Why would I do that?" *Unless it's because you were kissing Alicia last night and now you're here talking to me. You are a player, plain and simple.*

"I'm not sure." He reached out his hand. "Let's dance."

Eden considered his offer. The last time she danced with him, feelings began to flit around—feelings she didn't want to deal with now. "I think I'll finish this food."

Jeremy gave her a I'm-not-going-anywhere look with his raised eyebrows. "One dance."

Figuring he'd keep asking, she decided it'd be easier to dance with him and get it over with. She wasn't about to fall for any of his lines. She followed him out to the dance floor just as the music slowed and *Stay with Me* by Sam Smith began to play.

Jeremy took her in his arms and pulled her close. Too close. His woodsy cologne with hints of what smelled almost like basil circled her nose. The warmth of his cheek next to hers sent a shiver across her bare shoulders. Her resolve began to weaken. *Remember, he was kissing Alicia last night. Don't fall for any of this.*

"Where have you been?" he whispered into her ear.

"I've been around." Eden wanted to keep it civil, but distant.

"But avoiding me." His warm breath on her ear made her skin prickle.

"No," she lied. There was no reason to say anything about him and Alicia. It was really none of her business and it didn't matter.

He pulled his head back and peered at her, his eyes probing her for the truth. "Yes, you have been, and for the life of me I can't understand why."

She looked away from his intense gaze. "I'm not avoiding you." Why did he care if she was? He had Alicia.

"I don't believe you," he said.

"You can believe what you want." This conversation was going nowhere.

Someone tapped Eden on the shoulder. "Mind if I cut in?" Alicia asked.

Eden shrugged.

"I mind, actually," Jeremy said. "I'd like to finish this dance with her."

Alicia blinked, then scurried off.

Eden stared at him trying to figure out what just happened. *What is going on?*

"Are you going to level with me or not?" he asked.

They swayed to the music. Eden's heartbeat thundered in her ears and heat crawled up her neck. She sucked in a breath of courage and said, "Last night."

"Yes?"

"You and Alicia."

He drew his brows together. "What?"

She studied him. Did she have to spell it out?

"What about Alicia and me?" Jeremy watched her expectantly.

Eden didn't want to sound like she was in high school. "I figured that since the two of you . . ."

"The two of us what?"

Eden thought the other Sam Smith song *I Know I'm Not the Only One* would be more appropriate right now.

"Eden." He took a step back. "I have no idea what you're talking about."

Either he was clueless or he was a very smooth liar. "I overheard Alicia and one of the other bridesmaids."

"And?" He raised his eyebrows.

"They were talking about you and Alicia kissing." There she'd said it.

He dropped her hand and took a couple of steps backward. "They were what?" His voice was loud.

"Shhh," she said, bringing her finger to her lips. Eden didn't want some kind of scene on the dance floor.

He grabbed her hand and tugged her out a back door. Outside, they stood there with the ocean in the distance. "Tell me what happened," he said.

"While we were getting our facials, I overheard Alicia saying how the two of you were kissing last night."

He blinked a few times. "And you believed her?" He seemed insulted.

"Why shouldn't I?" She stood firm. "Since I'd seen the two of you pretty cozy at the restaurant last night—"

"You saw us at the restaurant?"

"Yeah. I lost my bracelet and I came back down to see if anyone had turned it in and I saw the two of you together." There wasn't any way he could deny what she saw.

After a few moments, he leaned in. "Did you see Alicia throw water in my face?"

"What?" Eden hadn't seen that.

Jeremy peered at her. "After I told her I wasn't interested."

"You told her that?" It wasn't hard to imagine Alicia's reaction, and Eden pursed her lips to stop the smile that wanted to break free.

"Of course." He pointed at her then back to himself. "You didn't feel a connection between us?"

She wasn't sure what to say. Her thoughts and feelings were all looped together into one massive knot.

"I know you felt it." He stepped closer to her.

"Maybe." Was the air disappearing? Because it was getting way too difficult to breathe.

He took another step toward her, which sent her heartbeat into a frantic thrashing inside her chest. "You think I'd be kissing Alicia, or any other woman?"

"I don't know." She'd only just met him.

"You don't?" He brushed a tendril of hair from her face, leaving a trail of warmth on her skin.

"Do I?" Confusion circled her mind. So much so, she wasn't even sure of her name.

"Let me be clear." He grazed her cheek with his finger as he gently ran his fingers through her hair. "I'm not interested in talking to, hanging out with, or kissing any other woman."

"You aren't?"

He tugged her close to him and every part of her yearned to feel his lips on hers. She let her gaze slip to his mouth, then she looked into the beckoning depths of his chocolate eyes. "I'm interested in you. Is that clear enough?" he said.

She nodded, her lungs devoid of any air now.

He leaned in and she could smell the cinnamon on his breath and feel the heat of his lips as they hovered over hers for what seemed like an eternity. *Kiss me before I die of anticipation.* He delicately pressed his mouth against hers as she collapsed into his embrace. Together, their lips mingled in a graceful, elegant dance. Soft but certain, he intensified the kiss and she followed suit, every muscle in her body quivering.

When he pulled back, he said, "Wow, that was even better than I imagined."

She steadied herself against the railing because her legs felt like they'd give out at any moment.

"Now are you convinced?"

"Yeah." She looked at him. "But where do we go from here?"

He shrugged. "I don't know. I only know I haven't ever met a woman like you and I'm not going to let you get away."

Eden swallowed hard.

"Sophie's going to throw her bouquet," a female voice announced over the sound system. "All the bridesmaids need to come in here."

"That means you," Jeremy said.

Hesitantly, Eden walked back into the building with Jeremy following her.

Eden lined up with the other bridesmaids and some other women.

"Throw it right here," Gabrielle said, taking a stance.

"No way, Gabs. I'm going to catch it," Alicia said. She threw a dirty look Eden's way. Eden gave her a smile.

Sophie shaded her eyes from the spotlight that was on her. "Where is Eden?" she said.

Eden raised her hand slightly.

"It's coming to you." Sophie laughed. She turned her back to the group of women, then tossed the bouquet over her head.

Alicia reached for it, but Gabrielle pushed her to the side, then tripped. The bouquet landed in Eden's hands.

"Who caught it? Who caught it?" Sophie said as she turned back around.

"Uh, I did," Eden said.

Sophie rushed to her and hugged her. "That means you're the next one to get married."

Eden just stood there, holding the bouquet, not sure what to say. Catching the bridal bouquet didn't actually mean anything. Did it? A small part of her kind of hoped it did.

"We're going to cut the cake now," Sophie said. She walked toward the table where an elegant cake sat atop.

"That's only a superstition," Alicia said as she passed Eden. "Doesn't mean you'll get married." Alicia cackled.

Eden looked down at the bouquet in her hand and for a moment, she was tempted to pummel Alicia with it. Instead, she followed Sophie.

Jeremy found her and said, "Good catch."

"I literally stood there and it fell into my hands." Eden put the bouquet on a table.

They watched Sophie and Antonio cut the cake, then feed each other. Eden laughed when Antonio got a little carried away and smeared some on Sophie's face.

"They really are a perfect match," Jeremy said. He reached out and grabbed Eden's hand. "That doesn't happen very often."

She gazed at him, her heart skittering. "No, it doesn't."

Jeremy leaned in and gave her a tender kiss on the cheek, making her heart melt. She wanted nothing more than to know this man better and see where things might go.

When Eden looked up, she could see Alicia across the room. Alicia spotted them and scowled. Eden scooted closer to Jeremy, then gave Alicia a simple smile. Turns out, all of Alicia's trickery and deceit backfired on her. In a way, Eden felt sorry for her and she hoped that Alicia would learn something from this experience—a relationship can't be built on anything but the truth.

"Thank you, everyone, for sharing this wonderful occasion with us. We're going to head out for our honeymoon," Antonio said. "I've kept it a surprise from Sophie."

Sophie grinned.

"Are you ready, baby?" he said to her.

"I am! Where are we going?" She clapped her hands together.

"I don't know about Soph, but this is killing me," Eden said. "Do you know?"

Jeremy shook his head. "Antonio is really building it up. I hope it's somewhere amazing."

Antonio held his hands up. "Pack your bags for a week-long adventure in Rome."

Sophie launched herself onto him. "Are you serious? Italy?" She started kissing him.

"That's so romantic," Eden said.

Jeremy turned to her. He cleared his throat, then said. "You know, my sister has been asking me to come visit her in Portland. I was thinking now would be a good time."

A warm feeling enveloped Eden. "Oh yeah?"

"You know anyone who could show me around?" He shrugged a shoulder. "Maybe find some great restaurants?"

The corners of her mouth turned up. "I think I know someone."

Jeremy pulled her close to him. He gave her a kiss that made her toes curl and sent an impulse of energy zipping throughout her body. Everyone and everything around them disappeared as Eden fully immersed herself in every bit of this kiss.

He pulled back, then rested his forehead against hers. "And maybe you know someone who can find the most romantic spot in Portland?"

"Only if you know someone who can serenade me with some original songs." Eden couldn't think of anything more romantic than listening to Jeremy sing his own songs.

"I think I can arrange that."

Eden reveled in his arms. She'd come to simply support her best friend on the happiest day of her life and never imagined she'd find a man like Jeremy—a man who made her believe in happy endings.

About the Author

Rebecca Talley grew up next to the ocean in Santa Barbara, California. She spent her youth at the beach collecting seashells and building sandcastles. She graduated from high school and left for college, where she met and married her sweetheart, Del.

Del and Rebecca are the sometimes frazzled, but always grateful, parents of ten wildly-creative and multi-talented children and the grandparents of the most adorable grandkids in the universe.

After spending nineteen years in rural Colorado with horses, cows, sheep, goats, rabbits, and donkeys, Rebecca and her family moved to a suburb of Houston, Texas, where she spends most of her time in the pool trying to avoid the heat and humidity. When she isn't in the pool, she loves to date her husband, play with her kids and grandkids, swim in the ocean, eat Dove dark chocolate, and dance to disco music while she cleans the house.

You can join her Reader News to keep up with her crazy life, including her newest releases, and receive your complimentary ebook, *Best Kind of Love*, at www.rebeccatalley.com.

Books by Rebecca Talley

ROAD TO ROMANCE

IMPERFECT LOVE

SPEAK TO MY HEART

ADDING CHRISTMAS

BEST KIND OF LOVE

GROUNDED FOR LOVE

ON DECK FOR LOVE

FLIPPING FOR LOVE

Post a Review?

Please consider leaving a review on Amazon. If you have an Amazon account, you can go to the book description page and write a review for this book. Authors love reviews!!

Reviews help authors find new readers and help readers find new authors.

Thank you!

FREE Download

Will Brynn recognize the best kind of love when she sees it?

Best Kind of Love: A Reunion Romance Novella Kindle Edition
by Rebecca Talley ▾ (Author)
★★★★☆ ▾ 98 customer reviews

amazonkindle

"This was a fantastic story!"
Gina K.

"The chemistry between the characters is great..."
Karen G.

**When you join
Rebecca Talley's Reader News
you'll receive a complimentary copy
in your preferred ebook format.**

Visit www.rebeccatalley.com to receive your free ebook.